THE PRUMONT METHOD

TREVOR J. HOUSER

THE PRUMONT METHOD

Published by Unsolicited Press
Printed in the United States of America
First Edition

Attention schools, libraries, and businesses: this title can be ordered through Ingram. For special sales, email sales@unsolicitedpress.com.

For information contact:
Unsolicited Press
Portland, Oregon
www.unsolicitedpress.com
orders@unsolicitedpress.com
619-354-8005

Cover Design: Andrew Wicklund
Editor: Jay Kristensen Jr.
ISBN: 978-1-956692-49-5

For Rupert

"God exists since mathematics is consistent, and the Devil exists since we cannot prove it."

—Andre Weil

THE PRUMONT METHOD

1

When did I predict my first mass shooting?

It was late winter.

Summerville, South Carolina.

Only I had the wrong church. It was Baptist, not Presbyterian. This was just after my divorce and right before I quit my job in healthcare marketing. I was knee-deep in the Method at this point.

My roommates were Archimedes, Gauss, and Poisson.

Is it weird to say a bunch of famous dead mathematicians are your roommates?

—

It only took me five days. The Method, that is. Which is actually lightning fast to finish something of this magnitude. I mean, it's only thirty or forty-odd pages, which really isn't that much when you think about it.

The Abel-Ruffini theorem spans five-hundred pages.

Almgren's regularity theorem is almost a thousand.

—

For some reason, I drove there. To Summerville, that is. The very next day, in fact. It sounds silly, but the numbers came alive there, so to say. I felt I should pay my respects or bear witness in some way.

I guess in the excitement, I'd forgotten to bring a change of clothes. I just jumped in the car and drove south. Not that I was excited about all the death and tragedy, obviously. But I felt like my life suddenly had meaning in a way I'd never experienced before. Like when veterans say they never felt more alive than during a firefight. It's bloody and horrible and at the same time it feels like windsailing the Drake Passage in the nude.

Or something like that.

When I got to the church, I walked up to the impromptu street memorial as if walking to a grave.

There were flowers and balloons and a big sign that read, "Don't leave us, Jesus."

—

When I drive at night, I often think of Poisson and the others.

From town to town, I mean. Barstow. Osage Beach. Thief River Falls. Wherever the Method takes me.

I find when I drive at night there's more space to think. Your mind reaches out further. It's almost like you're not there. Just darkness and speed. Not that I plan it that way. To drive at night. For some reason, nighttime just tends to be when the Method spits out the next location. I think it's random, but perhaps there's a pattern in there somewhere. Almost certainly there is. There's always a pattern. There's always Jesus and patterns and celestial fuck ups. That's true almost anywhere.

—

When I'm driving between towns, another thing I sometimes think about is Charles Whitman. Or George Hennard. Or Seung-Hui Cho.

Whitman blamed his rampage on a brain tumor.

Members of Cho's church told his mother he was possessed.

Hennard rammed his pickup through the wall of a diner, then killed twenty-three people with automatic pistols.

One night, I looked up photos of Hennard's crime scene online.

It wasn't a good place to die.

Seventies airport carpeting. Fake hanging plants. There were cold bowls of chicken noodle soup and purses that would never be opened again for a stick of spearmint.

In a way, it reminded me of what I found behind the soda fountain in Buffalo.

The way it looked almost fake and heartbreaking at the same time.

—

I'm in a motel in Iowa right now.

I like motel rooms.

Aside from the fact I mostly live in them, I genuinely like what they have to offer. There's a beautiful Swiss-watch precision in their plainness. Single-serve coffeemakers. Little gunmetal ice buckets. They're like shimmering complications hidden inside a Rolex Oysterquartz.

The motel room I currently call home has a retro green and white color scheme, as if it were 1965, which is actually the year I was born.

Scottie Pippen and Björk were also born that year.

The Year of the Snake.

Lucky colors: light-yellow and black.

The coaster for my drink, on the other hand, is green and white like the rest of the room.

I take a sip from my Gold Phantom, which is mostly cognac, orange blossom honey, and pineapple juice. I watch the ice cubes dreamily tumble and readjust in the cognac. Then I look at what I am doing on the little motel table near the window that looks out over a leaf-filled parking lot and a dinged-up shed marked ONLY!

What I'm doing is writing my obituary.

In fact, I've been thinking about death a lot lately.

—

For a moment, feeling the cognac melt down to the center of me, I imagine bullets entering my spleen and left eyeball. Where will they end up? In my back? Somewhere rolling around my navy-blue sweater vest? Will they go all the way through me and graze some nearby innocent bystander's serratus anterior so that they never forget what I did that day and name their firstborn son after me?

—

My name is Roger, by the way.

—

Gold Phantom:

1 ½ ounces VSOP cognac

2 spoons raw honey

½ ounce Licor 43 original

¾ fresh pressed pineapple juice

½ ounce fresh squeezed lemon juice

1 pinch salt

—

Roger is not as popular a name these days. As a matter of fact, it's currently ranked only 636th in popularity. That's according to the Social Security Administration. Also, according to them, the name reached its peak in 1945, coming in at #22. Right behind Frank and just after Raymond.

—

Frank is a museum.

Raymond is a deserted shipyard.

The Mateos and Cadens of the world will no doubt rule our iceless future.

—

How many fifty five-year-olds still feel young?

How many write their own obituaries in outdated motels?

How many of them have a college basketball game on in the background and can hear the announcer say, "Danny, it feels like the [insert losing team here] is beginning to lose contact," and take it personally?

—

When I was still at work, everyone became twenty years younger overnight, and they looked right through me as if I held no weight in their world. They trotted off to obscure taco trucks in laughing, hopeful packs. They talked incessantly via thumbs.

I watched them on the bus like they were rare giant albino manta rays. I watched them spiral and flare out to channel the world into their large unblinking eyes.

They were like a small piece of God no one ever expected.

Holy yet absurd.

—

This is three cocktail napkins' worth of my obituary:

> On June 18th, Roger "Rog" Prumont died of multiple gunshot wounds. He was 55.
>
> Rog happily practiced regional healthcare marketing for the last twenty-five years of his life. He had a passion for watching college basketball and occasionally sport fishing late at night. He was known to alternate between blade, peripheral-weighted, and mallet putters. He liked obscure whisky-based cocktails and women who performed illegal U-turns with a certain nonchalance.
>
> For many years, Rog liked wondering what he would've done at

the Battle of Hürtgen Forest. All that cold. All those trees. Potential best friends getting caught up in the treads of Panzers. "So goddamn cold," he thought he would've said to himself in some icy trench, if he'd only been lucky enough to be born earlier than he was.

Rog was best known for his quick wit and seemingly bottomless wet bar. It came with the Colonial-American house he bought at the apex of the 2008 buyer's market.

Rog liked to attempt casual Spanish on occasion.

In his spare time, he revolutionized mathematics.

Roger Prumont is survived by his ex-wife, Marion Talbot, 49, and their daughter, Zoe, 22.

A funeral service will be held this Thursday at (CHURCH TBD!) at 1 p.m. Flowers or donations are strongly suggested.

—

Obituaries tend to be two parts self-absorbed and one part idiotic, but they're also necessary. They tell the world what we like to think our lives meant. Not that it's the life I imagined for myself, but things have been going off the rails for a while now.

At least this time I am trying to embrace the freefall. I keep telling myself I can still steer in midair. Just think of all those skydivers.

They simply bend an elbow or dip a shoulder and—zoom—they're

over there!

Zip—they're

over here!

Why can't I do that?

2

I sometimes go to local schools.

I sometimes watch the children play soccer or something called "space fight" as I measure out steps across the back fencing.

I remember how my daughter Zoe used to play a game in the backyard where the porch was a pirate ship. She would dive off into the sun-beaten yard looking for lost treasure behind the stickers and Indian plums.

Sometimes I would sneak through the bushes behind her and jump out screaming, "Shark attack!" which sent her into a scurried-shock back to the porch, laughing and breathless.

That was the summer Zoe told me she loved without me telling her I loved her first. Unprompted love is rare like rhodium at that age. At least for a dad. I looked at her for a moment, waiting for everything to change, or for life to take it back somehow, but she just nodded and looked away as if she'd just seen her whole life mapped out in front of her and approved of it.

Just nodding and drinking her juice box.

"I love you, too," I told her, trying to be casual about it.

—

I don't just visit schools, of course.

Churches, community centers, movie theaters, casinos, bowling alleys, farmer's markets, malls. There are so many places to consider. This town has been easier than most. Some are too big, obviously. It's hard to pinpoint where you need to be, but this town is a nice size.

It always felt to me like a town of 10,000 is a perfectly nice size.

You have your high school football games. The summer fair with the casual meth heads. Plus, there's a decent enough chance people know your face so that you don't feel the need to cut them off in traffic and call them "fuckhead" as you barrel through a red light.

—

Like I said, the town I'm in right now is a town in Iowa.

There's a big lake nearby where I saw a bald eagle land on a Wendy's, but, in fact, it's called Little Lake.

Both the town and the lake, actually.

No one seemed to notice it but me.

The eagle, that is.

It dropped suddenly out of the sky like a laser-guided bomb and settled just above the cherry red electrified "W."

Then I went to the liquor store and bought some bourbon and grenadine to make a Kentucky Blizzard while going over some numbers.

—

Kentucky Blizzard:

1 ½ ounces bourbon

1 ½ ounces cranberry juice

½ ounce fresh lime juice

½ ounce grenadine

½ ounce simple syrup

orange half-wheel

—

It doesn't seem that long ago that I was still traversing the treacherous landscape of regional healthcare marketing, but now I'm crunching perceived grievance rates while dropping an orange half-wheel into a perfect storm of bourbon and fruit juices.

Not to say I'm some great mathematician.

I'm not by any stretch.

But I do like numbers. I like research. Even when I was a kid, I could see the point to numbers. The way they looked on a page made sense to me. But then I lost track of them somewhere around high school. Then I got married and had a family. I got deeper and deeper into my "career."

—

Things I used to write: "We specialize in team-ology," or "Your weight-loss program will see you now." Then, a week or two later, I'd see the words up on a downtown billboard or in the Sunday paper. At those moments, I wanted to be lowered into a bear cage slathered in elk blood. I wanted to light myself on fire and walk into a conference room, my melted flesh dripping all over the audio-conferencing system while calmly writing on the whiteboard, "Our prognosis? Convenience matters."

—

How did I rediscover numbers?

I guess it was at my fifty-fifth birthday party when my wife of twenty-five years told me she'd been having an affair with Kevin the Real Deal Realtor.

That was his actual name. Or his professional realtor name, anyway. It was on billboards and park benches all over town. He'd recently closed a sale just down the street from us. And now here he was in my life because of decisions I did or did not make. Or maybe decisions I didn't even know about.

—

I recall Zoe asking me why I was crying.

I wanted to tell her I felt like I was in the flame-engulfed engine room of a submarine that's just hit the biggest iceberg ever recorded, but I only gulped air instead.

We were on the front porch with the chipped gray paint.

We were beneath the old chestnut.

It was the set of a beloved, long-running TV show, seemingly on the verge of a devastating cancellation. I wanted to say something, but my lungs had nothing in them. There were no spaces in them to form words or even to breathe. I looked at her as if I were a living death mask. A gasping monument to the last night we would ever be the same people who took trips to San Diego together, and smiled across the yard at one another, steak-smoke and fluttery post-shark attack laughter filling the evening sky like fireflies of not feeling shitty.

—

I remember it was then that I wanted to disappear.

But that's not the right way to say it.

Not to disappear exactly, but to somehow shed my entire exoskeleton. To become a new and improved Rog. The latest model, impervious to failure and disappointment. But how? I thought numbers might have something to do with it.

But I had no idea about the motels yet.

I had no idea about the Blue Knights of Buffalo, or how many of them would die beneath the soda fountain.

—

"We're not the same people anymore," Marion told me, cleaning up after the guests had gone as if she were also sweeping up the shards of our marriage. "Or I'm not. Maybe the problem is that you're still the same. Did you ever think about that?"

—

How do you answer that?

"I want to start over as a wide receiver for the Cincinnati Bengals?"

"I will now commence the burning-of-the-neighborhood-to-the-ground by sounding a conch, signifying the beginning of a new civilization?"

—

At first, I focused mostly on things like probability theory, or more specifically the Poisson Distribution theory, which was invented by the French mathematician Siméon Poisson. In any case, it's useful in modeling events such as patient arrival intervals at emergency rooms or the meteorite strike frequency on Earth.

Except the theory—or method—I began working on had to do more than just predict when.

It had to tell me where.

It had to tell me who.

—

Did Baron Poisson have to write his own obituary? Did he get pressured by the CMO of a regional healthcare system to come up with the "Better You" campaign, which consisted mainly of embarrassing TV ads depicting stuffed animals racked with depression and some dude in a leotard talking about Stage 3 testicular cancer? All while his wife had a three-month affair with Kevin the Real Deal Realtor?

—

Poisson came up with something called celestial mechanics and his name was one of seventy-two inscribed on the Eiffel Tower. He ate lunch with his wife Nancy outside the Bureau of Longitudes and probably told her in the dying sunlight that she looked like a transcendental number.

—

You think it's easy to leave your home and your job and your wife of 23 years?

Actually, it is surprisingly easy.

I dare you to sit in your used Saab in front of your fucked-up porch and not briefly wonder: what's next?

3

Sometimes I eat outside. I leave the obituary and the lunar calendars and the mathematical scribblings in the motel room and go down to the pool with a pastrami sandwich.

No one hardly swims in it except for the boy from 109. I think he's in middle school, but it's so hard to tell with kids these days.

His name is Simon.

He talks about baseball and Star Wars between "epic" cannonballs into the deep end.

For the most part, I rarely talk to the people at the motels I visit.

I'm usually too busy anyway. Or I'm only there for a short time. But I've been here a few days already. In any case, today it's just me. Looking up at the high blue sky of spring. I think about calling Zoe on one of my burner phones, but then I decide against it. She'll get upset. She'll ask where I am and why I haven't come home. She'll say things about Marion I don't wish to hear.

—

Poisson had four children. But I believe his family life was quite happy.

The German mathematician Carl Gauss, on the other hand, had a wife who died very young, sending Gauss into a depression from which he never recovered.

That said, he still managed to teach himself Russian.

Not to mention, he was the first to prove quadratic reciprocity.

What did I do?

I'm living in motels and using burner phones.

My only friend is a tween in a Chewbacca t-shirt.

—

Sometimes, when I feel depressed, I fix myself a Death in the Afternoon and lie on the couch looking deep into the cryptic pattern of the green and white wallpaper, thinking about Marion or the soda fountain in Buffalo with the blood all over it, or sometimes, if I'm lucky, I think about nothing at all.

—

Death in the Afternoon:

1 ½ ounces absinthe

4 ½ ounces champagne

—

Buffalo was the closest I ever came to proving my theory. I mean, in some ways it did prove my theory.

I've been close a few other times.

There was that time I was in Kansas City and then it happened one state over outside Decatur. Or the time I knew it would happen on the California coast at 11:47 a.m., but I got the town wrong.

In Buffalo, I had everything right down to the exact community college, but while I waited outside the library doing my breathing exercises, I heard the pops come from somewhere else on campus.

It took me awhile to find the school's theater, but when I got there, it was all over. There was blood, but no screaming.

The loud bangs had stopped.

Just as sirens began to squall in the distance—that's when I found them, under the soda fountain in the concession area.

It looked like a multicolored cord of wood, but as you looked closer you could see hands, elbows, hair.

I could only see one face, but the face didn't look like a face. It looked like a cheap replica of a face you might find in a B-horror movie or in a Halloween costume shop.

I remember in the middle of the pile was a girl's green sweater. She must've been about Zoe's age. There was a curl of blonde hair just over the top of the collar where you could see her neck bending unnaturally to the left.

After quickly checking to see if anyone was still breathing, I left before the police arrived.

—

I often wonder about the girl with the green sweater.

For some reason, I imagine her inhaling helium after lunch and singing "Swing Low, Sweet Chariot," the way my first girlfriend in middle school did. Of course, she didn't know she was my girlfriend because I was too afraid to talk to her. She used to say she loved karate and dancing alone so no one better ask her to dance, or else. She went to the Sawtooths every summer. She had blonde hair. The same blonde hair as the girl in the green sweater. Did the girl in the green sweater like to dance? Did she like to sing? That's something I'll never know.

4

My theory doesn't have a name, but for a while I thought it needed one. Like the Prumont Theorem or the Prumont Conjecture, but after what I saw in Buffalo, I didn't care as much about what it was called.

I guess I just call it the Method now.

I'm not sure I even really meant to invent the Method. I'm not sure what I was thinking. I just locked myself in the study the morning after finding out about the Real Deal and started jotting things down. I'm not very political, but I suppose guns were front of mind because they had been in the news a lot lately. I mean it's impossible to watch those families hold it together in front of the TV cameras and not feel something. I can't really point to any other reason. Maybe it was subconscious. All I knew was I was unhappy. The numbers just appeared.

—

Of course, fortuitous mistakes in math happen all the time.

A quantum physicist, whose name I forget, came up with some equations about subatomic particles, but they only made sense if some mysterious particle existed, which it did, but nobody knew it yet. It was a quark. Or something like that. Dark matter, maybe.

Probably also a Frenchman.

In any case, he was ahead of his time. So just because people don't know about something doesn't mean it's not true.

Maxwell's equations predicted radio waves.

The planet Neptune was discovered by realizing an equation was right and the universe was wrong.

—

Perhaps the best instance of a happy mathematical accident was the case of Tamar Barabi. In 2016, she turned in her math homework and the teacher told her the method she used to solve the problem didn't actually exist. After writing up three proofs and a series of conclusions, Tamar sent the theorem to experts around the world and they confirmed that she had discovered a new geometric theorem. I believe it's called Tamar's Theory or something along those lines. Think about that. Sixteen years old.

—

I tried to tell Zoe about the Method, but she just breathed deeply on the phone as if I'd called up to say I had joined a yoga death cult.

"Where the fuck are you, Dad?" she asked finally. "Mom feels horrible. I think she's worried about what you're going to do. Dad? What are you doing?"

"Hey, Blueberry, I just have some work to do and I'll see you soon."

Blueberry is my nickname for her because when she was little she'd lay waste to entire cartons of them in one sitting. Plus, her head was almost perfectly round as a child. Like a bowling ball with big blue eyes, though she always insisted they were hazel, which I'm sure must've been another early symptom of her ODD. Not that we ever officially had her diagnosed or anything.

Some things you just know.

"Dad, I miss you," she said in a small voice that confirmed she was still my Blueberry.

"Miss you, too."

"What about Mom?" she asked.

"Ask her how the Real Deal is treating her."

Then I hung up as gently as I could.

5

Shooter profiles. Weapons. Dates. Weather. Times of day. Victim demographics. Financial and job market trends. Drug abuse and neurological disorders broken down by states, cities, and towns. Various types of venue.

Basically, all these things help the Method assess the likelihood of where the next mass shooting might occur.

Other people have tried it.

The CDC. Some kids at Stanford. But mostly they're looking for symptoms. They're searching for behavioral patterns the public or police departments can be on the lookout for.

The Method's main purpose is to pinpoint the exact location of the next shooting.

Except it's incomplete.

And in a way, it's hard to even explain.

Not in the traditional sense, anyway.

—

A report from the Congressional Research Service in 2013 defines a mass shooting as three or more killings in a single incident. So that's my criteria. For now, the best I seem to be able to do is get a couple things right like the day and the region. Or the time and the state. And then, if there's time, I improvise from there. I stay in that area up until the Trigger Event. The Trigger Event being what I call the exact moment the shooting begins. In any case, until that point, I walk the neighborhoods. I scout out the schools and the stadiums and other soft targets.

I see probabilities everywhere.

I am a walking calculator.

—

Here's a thing I do.

Once I've analyzed the output and the Method points me in whatever direction it points me in, I go to the middle of whatever town or city or backwater and just watch.

Usually, this is a park or square of some kind.

Sometimes it's just Main Street.

What I do is find some place where I'm out of the way enough to just stand or sit there and observe.

I watch the people on their phones or leisurely getting in and out of their cars. I watch businesspeople walk to lunch, laughing. I watch policemen writing traffic tickets or just staring dumbly from their black and white cruisers. I stand there in the hot sun or the softly falling snow thinking I am the only one who knows.

Nobody else has any idea in the slightest.

Except, of course, for one other person (or sometimes maybe two), but maybe they don't even really know yet.

It could be just a couple days away, although sometimes it's as long as two weeks out. Nevertheless, at some point in the near future, the routine will be disrupted, maybe even permanently. No one will walk. Some won't get phone service. Many will stay home. A few might even be affected directly.

Their children perhaps. Or their husband.

Or maybe, it will happen in that very spot where I'm standing. Just under that elm or behind the courthouse.

And perhaps there will be bodies like the bodies in Buffalo. The way they looked broken and unreal. As if you'd taken one of those giant stuffed animals you win at the carnival and violently threw it down a flight of stairs. Then it just froze there forever.

Their legs crossed unnaturally. Their stuffing coming loose around the belly.

Either way, the noise will be deafening.

Then silence.

Then cries and moans.

Then vigils and news vans.

Then maybe a statue or a plaque if it's truly horrific.

But unlike Civil War battle sites, people tend to forget what happened in these places. They will become sacred only for a few.

Then it will happen somewhere else.

The noise, followed by the cries and moans and necks bending unnaturally, etc. etc.

—

Charles Whitman. Mark Essex. James Huberty. Eric Harris and Dylan Klebold.

I think about them as I walk through the grocery store near my motel. Like a song you despise, but for some reason can't get out of your head.

—

Pythagoras said there was music in the spacing of the spheres, whatever that meant.

Currently of more importance is finding some good tortilla chips. I need something appropriately salty to go with my Juan Collins later in the evening.

—

Juan Collins:

1 ½ ounces tequila

1 ounce lemon juice

½ ounce agave nectar

2 ounces club soda

lemon, lime wedge garnish

—

The racist butcher. The jilted construction worker. The mopey high school kid in the deli. There are numbers behind every one of them stacked like bodies under soda fountains. They could all do it. Football watch parties. Interstate 20. Nothing is sacred.

—

One thing the Method has never gotten right is the shooter. The name, that is. I've gotten the race. I've gotten the financial background, their weapons, their grievances. But never an actual name.

—

One would think getting the weapon right wouldn't be that difficult since so many of these things involve AR-15s, but the Method has given me other guns, too.

The Mossberg 500 pump-action used in Oxnard.

The Winchester bolt-action in West Mifflin.

Of course, it doesn't always get that part right. Like the time the Method was convinced a Besa machine gun as the probable weapon of choice, which is a rare belt-fed gun that was usually mounted on armored vehicles in World War II.

I made some adjustments after that.

Not that it matters. I mean, to me it doesn't. Not in the end, anyway.

—

I shot a gun once myself.

I was in Vietnam.

Not the war, obviously. It was a vacation with Marion. This was probably the last one before the Real Deal got a secret shampoo hand job in our shower while I did my first and only Zumba class.

It was just outside of Saigon, which is now called Ho Chi Minh City. One of those unfortunate renamings like Yusuf Islam or Jefferson Starship.

In any case, it was just before I got horribly sick from food poisoning and spent two days puking in the hotel overlooking Bến Thành Market.

We were visiting a shooting range in the jungle complete with old Viet Cong bunkers and tunnels. You could shoot whatever. M16s, AK-47s, M60s. Just twenty bucks a head. The guns were bolted down to big concrete blocks so no one cartoonishly lost control and sprayed a tour bus with 600 rounds per minute.

What I remember most is how loud they were. Loud in the way that you feel it in your colon. I didn't even shoot the M60 because it was being hogged by some teens from Wisconsin, but the M16 gave out plenty of noise and violently smacked sand in the distance as I completely missed the target.

The noise made me feel sick, actually.

How did Charles Whitman do it for so long? Not hitting sand, but cars and skirts and thigh bones.

I pretended to have a good time, but all I could think about was dozens or even hundreds of young boys going at it with these things deep in the jungle and feeling nauseated and overwhelmed.

No wonder they did heroin.

No wonder they listened to the Carpenters.

—

Surprisingly, I come from a "gun family."

My dad and my brothers hunt birds. My grandparents shot at deer and elk together, then smoked and drank in great canvas tents along the Culiacán. Everyone in my family going back to somewhere in the Netherlands shot at things to smoke and grill.

Perhaps in 's-Hertogenbosch or Oudewater.

Anyway, it was a rite of passage.

—

My dad took me out one morning when I was nine years old. He shot at a flock just passing over a corn field we hid in. The smell of the spent shells cut through the funk of wet autumn leaves. Then he smiled. He sent our dog into the freezing water. When he came back with a dead duck in his mouth, I told my dad my feet hurt from the cold and he took me back to the car. He turned on the heat and rolled his eyes when I asked how much longer.

There's a thirty-nine percent chance his love for me dropped by almost half that day.

But math is tricky when it comes to things like love.

—

Do you know that moment when everything changes?

Do you know that moment when the shark latches onto your leg and your future Thanksgivings become the thing of percentages?

I know that moment.

I know percentages.

6

Over the past few months I've been in motels in Saginaw, Phoenix, Salem, Fort Lauderdale, and Spokane, to name a few. In fact, the time I went to Spokane was the quickest turnaround I've ever had using the Method.

According to my calculations, the Trigger Event was only eight hours away.

I was in Houston at the time.

Typically, I like to drive to the locations. I like to take in the sights along the way—stretch my legs—really see the country after so many years of not really getting around much because of the nature of my work and because Marion really didn't like to travel other than our honeymoon and that time in Vietnam.

But in this case, I had to park my car in a 24-hour lot and get on the next flight to Spokane. There weren't any nonstops, so I barely got in with an hour or so to spare after a connection in Seattle. By the time my taxi arrived at the biggest high school (which is always a good bet in a pinch) there were reports that something happened in Grand Rapids. Also a high school. I'm not sure why the location that time was so far off. But, of course, that was early on. I'm rarely that far off now.

—

I should mention that everything is intensely beautiful in the days and hours leading up to it.

Or maybe "beautiful" is the wrong word.

It's more like things are brighter, more vivid.

It's like the way surfers talk about the moment just before they get bitten by a great white. The reef stood still. No fish. The moon had synchronous pull. It's a sort of heightened self-awareness and attention to one's surroundings that most people don't get to experience, except probably in times of war or terminal illness. Even now, after all these times, the feeling is the same for me. A sort of sad excitement. Or an excitement tempered through a prism of sadness, if that makes sense.

The sunlight breaking through skyscrapers at sunrise.

Birds rising in black unison off a lake.

These moments feel sacred or endangered in some way. Like seeing a Canadian lynx or a switch-hitting first baseman. It's not a feeling I ever got from healthcare marketing. Or marriage, for that matter. Except the night she told me about what happened. That's when everything seemed more alive than they ever had.

—

Seven.

That's how many people were killed in Grand Rapids that day, if you were wondering.

Two shotguns and an unused pipe bomb.

47-year-old white male.

59 degrees and partly cloudy.

—

Last spring, I saw on the news one night how a man disarmed a shooter at a state fair and became an overnight hero. He was a gym teacher and part-time assistant football coach. His name was Randy. Everyone saw the interview outside his broken mobile home, but Randy was now suddenly far above things like adequate housing and dodgy retirement investments.

He was the guy who disarmed the shooter.

Randy saved lives.

His daughter looked up to him.

His legacy was preserved forever in the amber of that day.

Randy's eulogy would mention nothing of back taxes or wasted youth.

He was like an instant Chuck Yeager.

He was a Randy for our times.

—

The difference between me and Randy is that I don't intend to survive. In fact, it would be against the whole point.

—

Last spring was the last spring of my former life. The life before Kentucky Blizzards and Poisson. The life where I pretended everything would be okay. The life where I read the paper and had bimonthly dates with my wife. The one where we'd grow old together and go to Morocco for an entire month and never have to talk about what realtors named Kevin maybe did or did not do with the shampoo in our shower.

—

There were no surprises, only undercurrents and emotional weather patterns to set your watch by. Each day simply appeared. Like the Sunday edition of the *Times*. Except, one day, someone poured kerosene on the *Times* and it came crashing through the front window.

"Fuck you!" screamed the paper boy.

—

I see the boy at the pool.

Henry's his name. Not Simon.

I somehow got his name wrong the first couple times I met him. In any case, he arrives in trunks and carrying a water gun while I'm scanning the local newspaper for concerts and other upcoming large public events.

"So, Rog, do you live here, too?" asks Henry.

"No, just visiting," I tell him. "Do you live here?"

"Just for a little while. My mom is getting a new house with her sister. What is that you're drinking?"

"A Self-Starter," I say, almost forgetting I had it there.

"Is that like beer?"

I nod as I take a sip, gin shot through with a jolt of sunny Lillet.

"Sort of."

"My mom likes beer. You should come over and have a beer with her."

"Maybe I will."

Henry fills his water gun and happily shoots out a long steady stream against the shed marked ONLY! Only what, exactly? The rest of the sign is faded from too many summers. We'll never know.

—

Self-Starter Cocktail:

1 ½ ounces gin

¾ ounce Lillet Blanc

¼ ounce Giffard apricot liqueur

absinthe rinse

—

I look at my messages. Zoe, of course, who is relentless.

Also, the doctors called again. Or, I suppose, it's only one doctor. Or perhaps just the nurse. But I already know what they're going to say.

I told them I'm busy, but they still call.

I suppose that's comforting to know that they're persistent. Except that, in my case, it's just a pain in the ass. They'll call again next week, too, probably. I keep thinking about changing my number, but I don't. I'm not sure if it's laziness or something else. Nostalgia? The idea that things could somehow return to normal?

—

I used to play a game with Zoe when she was little called "Dr. Killjoy."

I was Dr. Killjoy and had an umbrella that doubled as a sword.

Zoe was a magician named Lizzie who could communicate telepathically with animals, specifically, for some reason, jaguars.

We would meet at my private club in London (our living room) and have "drinks," which were tumblers full of apple juice.

Then we'd travel via her bed to Morocco or Mt. Fuji or the moon. To do battle with mechanical sharks or zombies, which were actually the cats Marion bought on a whim, who I genuinely hated for many legitimate reasons, but that's another story.

"When will we play again?" Zoe always asked.

I wanted to live that life with her more than she'll ever know. Why can't that be possible?

It felt sad knowing why.

7

I like my motel room.

It's on the top floor at the very corner like I requested. It has bigger windows than most motel rooms I've been in. When I lie on the bed and look out the windows, the shed and the freeway just beyond the broken hedge disappear like Thorn's Catastrophe Theory.

There's only hackberry and quaking aspen swirling in the breeze out beyond the parking lot.

If you stood atop those trees, you could see all the way to the Walmart and the Indian casino across the lake.

Then blue sky and satellites and a million ghosts of French mathematicians.

—

What would Poisson have thought of Walmart? Would he grasp it all in terms of quantitative data or would he just stare at the infinite variety of Cheerios and wonder to himself "What in the ever-loving fuck is Medley Crunch?"

—

Instead of Cheerios, Charles Whitman had sweet rolls and condensed milk on the day he climbed the clock tower in Austin.

Humid, 92 degrees, sunny.

25-year-old white male.

—

I never thought I'd like being alone so much. You live your whole life with people surrounding you at home and at work and suddenly you're alone in Little Lake, Iowa making obscure cocktails and predicting the future.

—

To celebrate my newfound aloneness, I make four or five obscure cocktails and order a cheeseburger to-go from across the street. I watch a basketball game on mute with Brahms blaring on my clock radio. I lie on the bed like a great dying starfish from some undiscovered sea.

When I wake up at three in the morning, all the lights are on and the clock radio is blaring Bon Jovi. My mouth is dry. My head pounds.

The whole next day I stay inside and sleep and watch the towering trees sway under satellite-less skies like my watchful, angry mother.

—

Zoe calls and I pick up almost instantly as if the Method had predicted it. I suddenly feel foolish for having dodged her the last couple days.

She asks if I'm okay and if this is really how I want to spend the rest of my life, driving around doing whatever the hell it is I'm doing.

"It's hard to explain, Blueberry," I say.

"Please don't," she whispers angrily, meaning she's somewhere at work.

"Okay, sorry."

"Why are you not answering your phone?"

"I've been busy."

"I'm sorry about the last call. I just get upset about all this. About you and Mom. I'm worried for you."

"For me? Don't be. I just need to do this right now."

"Will you talk to Mom?"

"You can tell Marion I'm doing just fine."

"I told her you need space, but now she's talking about getting a private eye or something to find you. She's driving me crazy."

"You and me both."

Zoe laughs. She still wants things to go back to normal, but I don't know how to break it to her.

"You know I could find you if I really wanted to," she says.

"I know."

Zoe's a reporter back home. She probably knows how to track my phone or my credit cards or some other journalistic trick. I remind myself to use cash more often from now on. Naturally, I don't want her to find me, but I'd be proud of her if she did.

"I've got to go now," I tell her.

"I love you, Dad."

"Love you, too."

—

When did I become someone to be worried about?

The summer of my junior year in college, I drove down to Mexico and found work at a motel mending fence and bartending. One day, I drove a "gas truck," which was just a fucked-up Ford F-150 with barrels of gasoline strapped to the flatbed with old bungee cord. The percentage for tragedy was high.

Except they didn't trust a gringo with their money, so they sent an old local named Bancha with me. He brought a six-pack and drank and smoked as we drove, tossing his butts out the window, which flickered and tumbled at great speeds over the gas-soaked rags sticking out of our barrels like economy-sized roman candles.

He only spoke to me in English once the entire drive.

"This is the most dangerous highway in all of Mexico," he said, looking bored.

Of course, now it's clear to me.

The most exciting thing that ever happened to me was the equivalent of regional healthcare marketing for Bancha.

—

A drunk Floridian in Mexico once told me this story:

"A plane is going down over the Pacific when Death appears. He grants every passenger on the plane one day back in the time of their choosing. Wedding, childbirth, Game 7 of the '47 World Series, whatever. They can relive that one day before returning to the falling 737 where they all must die.

"Only, when the time finally comes, Death is distracted, and he forgets to bring one of them back to the plane diving into the ocean. Instead, that person wakes up after his wedding night. He's living in the past from that point forward and must find a way to live a more complete life knowing he only has so much time.

"But, as the date of the crash looms closer, he begins to wonder if he can't alter the outcome of that fateful day. Does he enjoy life to its fullest or does he tirelessly devote his life to thwarting his future death, risking happiness and the possibility that he only fails in the end anyway?"

"Are you Death?" I asked the Floridian.

8

According to my calculations, I have eight days to go.

So far, I have the city and the day. The time is changing every twenty-four hours, but it seems like it will be a late morning.

I don't know who.

I don't know where.

But it's a small town.

9

Marion hails from a Viking cul-de-sac somewhere in the Great Lakes area. Ice-scorched tundra. Swarms of semi-albinos politely borrowing lawnmowers from each other while dodging hornets the size of spark plugs.

—

She was a high-powered attorney for a few years, but she despised it. Motherhood and my perceived ascendency in regional healthcare marketing gave her the excuse she needed. To retreat into the exotic world of occasional grant writing and midafternoon book clubs that reeked of Gewürztraminer.

—

I once bought a kimono for her birthday. She hated it, but the whole night we laughed as she did this geisha dance and bowed deeply whenever she got up from the couch. It would be another year before she got pregnant. It was light years before dinner dates would be conducted like Civil War reenactments. Searching for the muscle memory of whatever we had lost in transit to the present tense. Excavations of old feelings. Squinting at one another like we were artifacts from a lost and forgotten time. A time of great prosperity. A time that would be celebrated only in our dreams.

—

The first weekend we spent together was mostly in bed ordering takeout. I remember thinking to myself she smells like Switzerland. Switzerland has a smell. Like fresh laundry and rare minerals.

—

Marion and I actually went there for our honeymoon. Not many Americans go to Switzerland for their honeymoon. Outside the smell, all I remember specifically about Switzerland is how they—the Swiss—made very large sandwiches that went pretty well with Riesling. It was always very cold Riesling. I have decided very cold Riesling is one of my favorite things. In fact, Very Cold Riesling would be a perfectly good name for Gwyneth Paltrow's next child, or perhaps a strip club DJ.

—

I remember when we first went to our financial planner.

His name was Alan.

"Looking at your finances, I think it's safe to say you'll be working well into your seventies," said Alan. "Do you expect a raise or change of employment in the near future?"

He was looking at me.

"As long as I'm able to promote cancer awareness via sentient stuffed animals," I said with a straight face.

As I said this, I could see Marion was looking at some papers in front of her, imagining a different life where she was married to a duke or software designer who had a knack for fixing deck furniture. I looked at the papers, too. The papers were about how little money we had saved and why that meant we should probably go ahead and make spring break plans in Syria.

Marion was breathing in deeply and then exhaling. She did not look back at me.

"It's simple," said Alan as Marion was still slowly breathing in and out like a shock victim. "We need to decrease your spending and increase your savings."

The financial planner took a gleaming black-covered packet of papers from his briefcase. Across the table, solemnly passing it to us. Our death sentence.

"These are my recommendations," he said.

"Thank you," I told him, putting the packet in my satchel made of Venetian buffalo calf I bought using a Christmas bonus I was supposed to put into a Roth IRA.

Marion and I thanked Alan, then we got into the elevator and didn't speak. We walked out of the building in slow motion, and there was no noise. The world was ending somehow. My fiscal incompetence. The Middle East. Whatever the fuck Tom Cruise was doing. Then, one sound at a time, the street came back to life, and we were moving at full-speed again.

—

We didn't kiss goodbye.

It would get better, I told myself.

I waited for it to get better.

—

Sometimes, after dinner, I used to stick my hand down Marion's underwear and make her breathe heavily, but it wasn't long before she was mostly bathed in the glow of her computer.

"Not now," she would say.

"Bump uglies in the shower?" I would say.

She wouldn't laugh. Saying "bump uglies" used to make her laugh. Saying what used to make her laugh also didn't make her laugh. I sometimes went to bed by myself and watched historically inaccurate pornos about female ninjas, who, more than spying around feudal Japan, seemed mainly preoccupied with performing various sex acts on gabled roofs. "It's a time of great uncertainty," one of the feudal lords said atop a gabled roof after having probably historically inaccurate anal sex with one of the female ninjas.

—

"Kevin the Real Deal Realtor?" I blurted when I found out. I almost laughed, but then I didn't, because I could tell she was serious. There's a whole world out there most people will never see, I thought. A world chock full of Kevins and high-ivied walls and whispered stock tips at sun-dappled picnics along the Upper Housatonic.

—

Very quietly, Marion began to cry.

I kissed her neck, right where there is a small freckle. My freckle. Little sobs against my shoulder. Fluttery kisses.

She is perfect for me in so many ways, I thought.

—

"What are your financial goals?" the financial planner had asked with a straight face.

I looked out the windows thinking, *multiple homes in Bora Bora and the Azores. Crack orgies and buckwheat honey flown in daily.*

But all I did was look out the window at the building across the way.

Whose dreams were being crushed in there, I thought?

10

We used to laugh and have sex and talk about renting movies, imagining in the future one of us compromising a little more than the other, trading off on what movie we chose, which, in a way, in my mind, is what love is supposed to be.

11

Out of habit, I find myself at the local sporting goods store. I'm looking at assault rifles. Bushmaster AR-15s. Smith & Wesson M&P15s. Chinese-made QBZ-95s.

The Dayton shooter used an AR-15.

Nine dead and twenty-seven injured in just thirty-two seconds.

—

Scott Flansburg, aka "The Human Calculator," is faster than that. He can add the same number to itself more times in fifteen seconds than an actual calculator can.

—

"Do you want me to take anything down?" asks the clerk.

"Just looking," I tell him.

"You a hunter?"

"More of a hobbyist."

"I have just the thing," he says.

He gently lifts one of the assault rifles off its rubberized pegs and lays the gleaming black thing on the glass counter in front of me like he'd made it himself.

"The neat thing about this one is you can change its caliber and barrel length without any tools," he tells me.

"That sounds like fun."

"Damn straight, right?"

—

I find myself wondering more and more if I should be telling someone about the Method.

But who?

The authorities?

The New York Times?

The American Mathematical Society?

And even if I did, would they take me seriously, or would I just be yelling "Fire!" in a crowded auditorium when the fire is actually one state over? Or two?

I admit, one problem might be that I've yet to get it right. Certainly, I've gotten some things right. But never all of them. That's the key, obviously. I could've raised the alarm at the campus in Buffalo. Just because I was too far away doesn't mean there wasn't a security guard or brave lacrosse player nearby that could've intervened on my behalf. But maybe I just got lucky that time.

—

Of course, I couldn't have told anyone the time I was in Monterey, because, like I said, I was on the wrong end of the California coast.

The sirens were whining all over Oxnard that morning, but in Monterey, I was holding a peach in perfect silence. All you could hear were gulls and the Pacific.

No screaming.

No panicked running with baby strollers.

I waited for "it" to happen in the middle of the farmer's market for another fifteen minutes or so until the reports started streaming in online.

"Fourteen dead," said the Internet. "Ten-year-old boy among the victims."

I went back to my motel like a one-man funeral procession.

—

Relaxed tan cargo pants.

21-year-old white male.

75 degrees and sunny.

—

Fifteen or twenty years ago, I probably wouldn't have come up with the Method.

Life hadn't forced my hand yet.

I was making okay money. We had a nice white house with smart black shutters, plus good public schools and a handsome little pond within reasonable walking distance. But as the years ticked by, I realized how late we'd begun. We were living the life our parents had lived when they were in their twenties, except their parents had won wars and made Jimi Hendrix. I was well into my thirties when we started a family and my career began in earnest. Before that it was just a blur of paycheck jobs. Meanwhile, friends and cousins were ten years into dentistry or Exxon Mobil. By the time I got serious about regional healthcare marketing, they were building their own practices and destination wineries. They had condos in Eleuthera and gas dual hydrostatic riding mowers. They were talking about retirement the way I talked about dry cleaning.

It wasn't long before I realized we would never catch up to them.

Our lifestyle was an illusion that couldn't be maintained. At some point, the strain would prove too much. It would break apart in the icy atmosphere of reality and rain down until it was reduced to a feeble spray of fire and debris that no one would ever bear witness to.

—

One thing I never told anyone was that they were going to fire me. This was before the Method and the birthday confession. It never officially happened, but that's because I left before it could.

Now here I am in Iowa.

Now here I am having cocktails at a motel pool with middle schoolers.

—

How I found out was that I was cc'd on an email about it.

My own firing, that is.

"I think we're letting Roger go the end of next month," it said, matter-of-factly.

It was part of a larger email, but had this thrown in at the end. Almost as an aside.

"Sounds good to me," came the reply.

Of course, I didn't respond. I didn't say a word to anyone. I just pretended it never happened and hoped it would go away. I went to Subway and bought the 6-inch sandwich combo with a medium drink and chips. Then I went to the sports bar next door and swallowed a beer. I listened to NPR in my car. The people on the email must not have noticed because I ran into one of them on the elevator the next day.

"How're things, Rog?" he asked in a neighborly way

—

There's a very large mirror over the desk in my motel room. It's almost too big for the room, but gives the impression one is in a much larger room, which I suppose is the whole point.

Marion never liked doing it in front of the mirror.

Of course, sometimes, in rooms like these, when we were traveling to one of Zoe's lacrosse tournaments and undressing before bed, I would slap Marion firmly on the backside and exclaim, "Sweet mama!"

She neither laughed nor hit me back.

She would simply say, "That's enough, Rog."

—

Does she ever tell Kevin the Real Deal Realtor that it's enough?

—

So far, the main real estate I'm interested in around Little Lake are the schools.

I've visited the elementary school, middle school, high school, and charter school. You never know where it's going to happen, but schools have a high probability. Although businesses and restaurants tend to be higher, they're tougher to hash out with my equation. It's a blind spot I'm working on. Like so many other things in my life right now, the Method is a work in progress.

Einstein took ten years to perfect the Theory of Relativity.

Not that this is in any way on the same level. But it's important. Which reminds me, maybe I should come up with a better name than just the Method. Buffalo or no.

The Prumont Function?

Variables?

Estimations?

In any case, what the Method does is allow me to get close enough to run some ground-game on my own. I have to take what the Method gives me. Intuition and common sense are the backbone of all mathematics, in the end. I forget who said that. Or did I just say that? Either way, it's true.

Except, again, I guess it doesn't matter for those teenagers stacked beneath the soda fountain.

My equation didn't save them.

Maybe it won't save anyone.

Maybe its only purpose is to save myself or make me acceptable in some way.

It's hard to explain.

12

There was a short time just before Buffalo where the Method didn't work.

Of course, in a sense, it's never properly worked the way it's intended, but there was a brief period when it suddenly provided no locations or times or anything. At first, I was worried it had all been random coincidence. And then I started fiddling with numbers the way you might fiddle with the engine of a broken-down car.

But I found nothing.

For four weeks I found nothing.

Missing one shooting is one thing, but I missed five. One in Pensacola, one in Missoula, one in Durango, one in Altoona and another in Odessa. The one in Odessa had 11 killed and 17 injured. How could the Method miss that? It would be like the Hubble Telescope missing the Death Star.

In any case, I kept driving from town to town, just in the event it might change something. That the change of scenery might have an effect on things in some cosmic way. Forward momentum. Anything. It wasn't long before I found myself less interested in tinkering with the obituary and instead watching a lot of basketball in various Rust Belt motel rooms accompanied by Egg McMuffins and Alabama Slammers. I began to wonder if that's really all this was. Just me needing to get away from the home situation and then papering over that rather humdrum, borderline immature reaction to adultery with an incredibly complex and even somewhat romantic mathematical action movie.

But then, one morning, it worked again.

I was half-watching the Demon Deacons laying waste to the Wolfpack when the Method gave me Buffalo.

I almost choked on my Alabama Slammer when I saw it.

But there it was, clear as day. A date and the time and even a specific location within the city. Of course, it didn't tell me about the girl in the green sweater or how much blood there would be.

Even math has its limits.

—

Alabama Slammer:

1 ounce Southern Comfort

1 ounce sloe gin

2 ounces orange juice

garnish with orange slice and maraschino cherry

—

Before Buffalo, I was in Fort Wayne, which is just a day's drive. I remember driving along Lake Erie on the 90 and singing happily to a song on the radio, as if I were going to a wedding or a college reunion.

Sometimes, I forget what potentially will transpire in these places.

I imagine it's not unlike the way Steinhaus and Ulam approached the Manhattan Project. You get caught up in the excitement of the chase.

You don't think about the cancer passed from one generation to the next.

You don't think about the flesh being cooked off the bone.

13

I sometimes wonder: what if I'd instead created a mathematical theorem that predicted horse races or where Sharon Stone would be in a state of undress from 1983-1995?

Why mass death?

Why tragedy?

Of course, that wouldn't solve my death wish problem. And maybe, subconsciously, that was a reason why I discovered the theorem I did. But the path I've taken is a dark one. That said, I've felt more alive the past few months than ever before.

Besides, there is no Wikipedia page for regional healthcare marketing failures.

There is no cocktail named after a cuckold.

At least, I don't think so.

14

I run into Henry at the pool again.

"Do you want to play Marco Polo?" he asks.

"I think you might need a friend with a younger back," I say, instantly realizing it's one of those lame adult jokes that aren't even really jokes, but pathetic pleas into the abyss of who gives a shit.

I sit down on one of the old lawn chairs to noodle on some random variables, feeling like Archimedes taking in the last rays of Sicilian sunlight after a long day of founding hydrostatics.

"We're having tacos tonight," says Henry cheerfully. "My mom has lots of beer and said you should come over."

I surprise myself with how quickly I reply.

"What time?"

—

When she comes to the door, I can tell she didn't invite me. She asks if I want to sit down and pulls a laundry basket off the couch, quickly scanning the room for any other embarrassing debris of daily life. Then she goes down the hall where I can hear her whisper-arguing with Henry about what the hell a strange man is doing in their living room.

I look around. Their room is clearly bigger than mine. There's a bedroom somewhere. I can tell the couch is one of the foldout kinds.

"Do you want a beer?" Henry's mother calls from a kitchenette that's partly hidden by a green-cushioned partition.

"Sounds good," I say.

She returns holding out a cold can of Modelo, smiling politely, gamely attempting to engage some long-dormant hostess-mode. Medium-length flare of blonde hair. Turned up nose. She looks like Gretchen Corbett from *The Rockford Files* and *Emergency!*

"My name's Beth, by the way," she says. "So, I guess you know Henry?"

"We're both fans of the pool," I say. "And I'm Roger, but everyone calls me Rog."

"Well, Rog, are you here on business or visiting family?"

"What happened to vacation?"

"Vacation to Little Lake? You're hilarious."

—

We drink more beer. Henry blasts aliens while Beth fills our nostrils with ground beef and Old El Paso taco seasoning. I look out their window, but I can't see the trees or the pool. Though I can see my room on the third floor above the parking lot. Has Beth ever seen me? Can I see her?

"Do you want to play?" asks Henry.

I take the controller, but the aliens swarm and devour me almost immediately.

Henry can't stop laughing.

"That's the worst I've ever seen," he says.

—

I was always good with kids. I would build spaceships for Zoe out of delivery boxes and she'd explore the outer reaches of our backyard.

"Quick, get inside!" I would yell from the deck. "It's an asteroid field."

She would squeal as I pelted her cardboard vessel with old tennis balls.

—

Beth tunes the radio in the kitchenette to mariachi.

"Sorry, but we're pretty serious around here about taco night. Also, we're pretty serious about our math homework, aren't we Henry?"

"Right now, Mom?"

"Before dinner, mister."

"But math is boring!"

"Boring?" I say to Henry. "Did you ever hear of the Hairy Ball Theorem?"

"The hairy what?"

"It proves it's impossible to comb all the hairs on a tennis ball in the same direction without creating a cowlick."

"That's weird," Henry says.

"That's nothing. Did you know math is 50,000 years old?"

"So?" says Henry.

"So, the first math problems were done on animal bones."

"Whoa, that's gross."

I help Henry with his geometry, while Beth rinses and chops. "Thanks," she mouths from the stove.

—

Over dinner, Beth asks what I do.

"Healthcare marketing," I say.

"That sounds exciting," she says wryly.

"Oh, but it is. Integration of multi-channel tactics to drive engagement? ROI and KPIs? Hell, on a good day, I can increase strategic advantage in a hypercompetitive landscape."

"I'm sorry to hear that," Beth says, laughing.

"Me too."

—

For once, I don't think of Marion. I don't think of numbers or the marked increase in mass shootings along the Gulf Coast. I watch Beth lick sour cream off her pinky knuckle. I listen to the uneven braying of trumpets and accordions coming from the radio.

"Thanks for inviting me," I say to Beth as I step outside, the sun long gone.

"Any time," she says.

When I get back to my room, I pour a splash of whisky and work up the nerve to call down to their room.

"Hello," Beth says.

"Hey, me again," I say. "Rog," just in case she doesn't remember.

"That was fast. Did you forget something?

"Yeah, I did, actually. I mean, I forgot to ask if maybe, you know, we could go out for a drink or dinner one of these nights. Just in the neighborhood or something."

"You mean just the two of us?"

"Sure. I mean, if that's even possible. Sorry, I don't even know what your situation is really."

"Does tomorrow night work?"

15

On the TV, they are saying there's been a shooting in a honkytonk bar outside Dallas.

Three dead. Two others in critical condition. Shooter dead.

I give a wounded look at all the equations taped up on one wall of my motel room. How did they miss? How did they fuck up?

—

Not that I haven't missed before, but I thought that lull might just be an anomaly. Since then, I hadn't gotten a date wrong in weeks.

Was it six weeks? Five?

And I'd made alterations since then. Safeguards. The Method had been whittled down to its most efficient version.

—

It's only ten in the morning, so I make a Harvey Wallbanger.

To reset. Something with orange juice feels appropriate. As I measure out the Galliano, I wonder if the Method is somehow telling me whatever is about to happen in Little Lake will be bigger. Could the Method differentiate between big mass shootings and smaller ones? Or was there something in the data that made the smaller ones harder to detect? Or was it all completely fucking random?

—

Harvey Wallbanger:

1 ½ ounces vodka

4 ounces orange juice

½ ounce Galliano L'Autentico

garnish with orange slice and cherry

—

A part of me was worried about this possibility even in the beginning. The possibility of it all being random and pointless. Especially back then. But I couldn't stop myself. Besides, the den was a rather cozy lab. My well-worn Dixon leather chair with the brass studs. The bar cabinet with the big antique mirror-back. Massive picture window overlooking the hundred-year-old chestnut out front.

Every once in a while, Zoe would knock on the door and ask if she could come in. To hash things out over a drink or bring in a conciliatory plate of meatloaf from Marion and watch a little basketball on TV together.

But Summerville ended all that, of course.

It ended a lot of things for me.

For one, I don't go to church anymore. Not that I was a model churchgoer, but I suppose I believed in some higher power. At least around the holidays. Now things feel different.

That's when I sensed most of my life had a sort of fakeness to it. The numbers felt more real, more alive. The den and that house and my job are what felt made up. My life with Marion and those people who said things like "bounce rate" or "bottom-of-the-funnel." Who talks like that? Who had I become exactly?

—

Some mathematicians believe in God, but it's unprovable, in my opinion.

I'm not sure what Poisson thought of religion.

One of his passions, of course, was celestial mechanics, but his priorities were quite clear.

"Life is good for only two things," he said, "doing mathematics and teaching it."

—

When I'm older, I want to know that Zoe goes to the museum with friends and has tea in bed and visits Crete. I want to know her neck will never bend unnaturally. I want to know she will remember me.

—

Will you remember me, lady girl? Hey, Blueberry? This is your daddy, sweetheart. I'm a living man at this exact moment in history.

I'm your father.

16

Spring in Iowa is beautiful.

So many browns and greens and yellows.

It can be a mean world, so a little color is nice.

When the doctors call, when you're writing your obituary—when whatever—you should see things like spring in Iowa.

You should listen to Pastor T.L Barret & the Youth for Christ Choir.

You should make a soft-boiled egg.

Except, I guess it doesn't matter.

I sometimes think this is all kind of funny. I mean, it's incredibly sad, but my particular situation within the larger picture can sometimes feel that way. It's like when people come off their track, things look different. Or is it off their moorings? In any case, why do things in life tend to look so absurd from a different angle? It's like you've been shot from the moon without a rocket. The Pacific gets bigger and bigger beneath you. Eventually, you will make landfall. You know this. But until then, the sunlight envelopes you, and you feel warm all over, and things feel like they might just work out.

—

I spend the afternoon at a community center pretending to be interested in a basketball game. I try not to think about Dallas. Or why the Method missed.

It's just a glitch, I tell myself.

Everything will be okay.

I take a deep breath and look around for white males under twenty-five. That's as specific as the Method has been on this one. Then I let my mind wander and I think about dinner later with Beth. I think about how Zoe and I used to play pickup games at the Y down the street and then we'd drive home in my Saab 9-3, which, at that time, she called my 'ports car. It was used and had a dent on the driver side door, but to her it looked like a Ferrari Testarossa. I could've gotten a little Japanese sedan or something along those lines for a lot cheaper and it would've lasted longer. But I got the Saab instead. It felt like something my dad would buy. It felt like something I could drive to the country club I would never belong to and no one would notice the dent and how old it was if they didn't look too hard. That's something I practiced in my daily life, too. Walking around, hoping people wouldn't look too hard.

—

I overhear two moms talking about Dallas while they watch their kids play basketball.

"It feels like it's every day now."

"It's just so scary. So random."

"Isn't your uncle some kind of NRA guy or something?"

"You mean, Ken? He's a neocon nutjob, alright. I finally had it out with him at Thanksgiving. Just stop with all the Second Amendment, bullshit, I told him. You know what he told me?"

"What?"

"He said when the government collapses, you'll be begging me for a gun."

—

I don't know why I'm so obsessed with how people perceive me, but I am. I try to be as cold in my self-appraisal as *The New York Times* would be. "Failed Math Hobbyist Dies a Cuckold." "Underwhelming Healthcare Minion Succumbs to Injuries in Death-Match with Kevin."

I suppose I'm not one of those people who thinks life is subjective. Everything you do can be counted for or against you. I know some people are happy doing meaningless things and not leaving any sort of legacy, but no one can help those people. They're like moss. They're like the Black Sea. It's like everything that doesn't take into account the Law of Quadratic Reciprocity or Ric Ocasek.

I don't pretend to know why we we're put here on Earth, but flaming holy hell if just "being" is the reason.

—

That's why I'm here in Little Lake.

To prove that I mattered.

There are only two ways for a person of unexceptional means to instantaneously reverse their life's downward trajectory and erase all the previous years of fear and mediocrity:

Win the lottery.

Get shot in the face while trying to save others.

17

I fix myself a Bunker Buster and watch the news about that honkytonk bar. Out my window I can see that it's beginning to rain, so maybe taking Beth just around the corner to that little Italian place is a better idea than going all the way across the park and past the lake to the steakhouse. No one likes walking in the rain on a first date.

—

Bunker Buster:

¼ ounce vodka

¾ ounce strawberry schnapps

1 beer

—

Marion liked the rain.

In fact, the night I met her, we were both drunk and she danced in front of the headlights of her car in the middle of a downpour, which sounds like a tragedy in the making. And, in a way, it was. Only the tragedy took a very long time to develop, like a Proust novel or the Enormous Theorem, which was a mathematical proof that began in 1971 and was only just completed.

In any case, she just got out and started dancing in the middle of a parking lot. It was Stevie Wonder that she was dancing to. "Sir Duke."

I remember because it's one of my favorite songs.

There weren't any other cars around. It must've been close to two in the morning, but still. I fell in love with her right then and there. I even got out and danced with her.

—

Mathematics has all sorts of theories on love. Like anything else, love is a pattern. Constellations of affection. Systems of jealousy. If math can predict the weather or reveal the laws of the universe, why not the subatomic particles that define romance?

—

Game theory tells you the best way to pick up strangers in a bar.

The Drake Equation helped one lonely hearts mathematician discover he'd only find 10% of the women he met agreeable and only 5% attractive.

—

There's also something called the "negativity threshold." It's the point at which the negative effect of one person becomes so great that their partner can no longer diffuse the situation with their positivity.

Marion and I reached the "negativity threshold" long before she said things like, "I just don't know about us anymore." It was long before I moved into the den and drank margaritas for dinner.

—

"Yikes." That's something she also used to say. Marion's humor was dated in that way.

She liked ribeye.

She liked basketball on TV.

She liked so many things I liked.

Of course, Marion rarely danced these days. One gets older, obviously, but that wasn't the only reason. My overall attitude certainly didn't help.

Not to mention the doctors.

Not to mention Kevin the Real Deal Realtor.

—

In the shower, I watch all the soap run down my legs and into the drain. It reminds me of that scene from *Psycho*. The blood swirling around the drain. I imagine the blood in that honkytonk bar in Dallas. Maybe in the bathroom, or on the dance floor. Bloody handprints on the mechanical bull.

Although not as much blood as the soda fountain.

I think I blocked out just how much blood there was. I was mostly covered in it after I'd gone through the bodies, looking for a pulse or whatever else you look for in those situations.

When I walked back towards my motel, a medic even stopped me to see if I'd been hit, but everyone else left me alone. I was only a few blocks away, but it felt farther than that.

A little girl with her mom pointed at me.

She looked confused.

As if she wasn't entirely sure what life had decided to show her that day. The only thing I could think to do was give her a thumbs-up, which I did.

No doubt a vision etched in her brain forever.

The blood-covered man, giving a thumbs-up on the way back to his motel to take a long shower and drink all the whisky he could hold.

18

Beth answers the door like we've known each other since high school.

"Hi there," I say.

"Hi back," she says.

—

I'm a fifty-five-year-old-man going on a motel date.

In my room, taped above seventeen bottles of liquor, is a math thing that could change the world.

Somewhere Wikipedia is licking its chops.

—

What would Marion say?

I'm sure she would have an opinion.

"This is what happens," I would tell her calmly, but with intensity. "This is what happens to people who fuck random realtors and tell their husbands on their birthday as though they were explaining an unpaid parking ticket."

—

As we walk through light rain, Beth tells me about her son. She tells me he doesn't have many friends right now. She tells me, "Boys will be boys." She touches her neck twice.

Flirting? Or just neck pain?

She looks up at the night sky and takes a deep breath, so I do, too.

"Where are we going?" she asks, talking about the restaurant or bar, but sounding like something more dramatic. Marrakech? Canis Major?

We would be one of those couples everyone talks about.

"They found a second life running guns out of Bogotá. They went scuba diving naked every morning and smoked hashish after lunch."

Except, no one would say that.

Nobody wants to know where they've fallen short. Nobody has time to be properly jealous.

—

We are sitting in a dull red glow at the back of Mario's. I order the most expensive bottle of red, which is somehow only twenty-seven dollars. Something called California Blend.

"I'm almost divorced," she says, putting down the menu and breathing in deeply.

"Me too," I say, somehow just noticing she has on a very nice white sweater with midnight-blue fleur-de-lys all over it.

"Sorry, that sounded lame," she says.

"I sound lame all the time," I say. "Do you want to talk about it?"

"Hell no."

We eat the warm bread out of the basket and look at each other, smiling.

"Can I ask you something?" she says.

"Shoot."

"What do you know about little boys?" She groans and takes another sip of wine. "Jesus, that came out wrong. Am I on a roll or what? I guess I'm surprised Henry brought you to our place. Listen, he barely even talks to me these days. I think it's the separation and maybe school. Who knows?"

"Well, I guess it's easier to talk to them when you aren't in charge of them," I say. "I have a daughter who went through her fair share of phases, too. Well, she's older now, of course."

We talk about Zoe and Little Lake, but not about the impending disaster. It could alter the equation in some way. That's what I tell myself, anyway. I don't know really. I approach the whole thing like the quandary of time travel. The less I muddle, the purer the result. I tell myself this as our veal scallopini comes out and we order a second bottle of their finest California Blend.

—

Will I sleep with her? The question suddenly flaps in the breeze of my brain like a banner behind a fast-diving plane. Would it be my place or hers? But it would have to be mine. Because of Henry. Where will I put all the work up on the wall? Is there too much liquor on the bureau for a healthcare marketing professional? Have I done sit-ups even once this week?

—

A man walks up to us in the middle of dinner and says hello to Beth as if they know each other well. He smiles and gives me a quick hello.

"Well, have a nice dinner," he says, and then he's out the door.

—

"I think we should maybe go," says Beth, looking suddenly uncomfortable.

"You don't want dessert?" I say, feeling relaxed, like we've been together for years.

"No, I should probably get back. I don't want to keep my sister waiting like that."

I suddenly feel like the evening is getting away from me.

"Maybe we can take a walk if the rain's let up," I offer.

"Sure, a walk would be nice."

After asking for the check, we sit back and enjoy the rest of our wine. That's when I see Beth's eyes get large like the last hartebeest at the watering hole.

"Oh fuck," she says.

—

The man comes in aggressively from the front door. He is about my size, which is average, but his forearms look like pickup trucks. He has on a plaid shirt. His hair is smashed down around his ears most likely from the ten-gallon Confederate hat currently resting on his skull-shaped gearshift.

"Well, isn't this a fucking sight," he says to the restaurant.

"So, Bob did call you," Beth says, drinking down her glass of wine. "Why is it all your friends are assholes?"

The man with pickup arms expresses zero concern with Bob's purported role in the situation and snorts like a bull instead.

People are looking now.

The waiter is frozen a few feet away with the check.

"I've been looking for you, you know?" he says, still not recognizing my existence. "You won't answer your phone."

"Excuse me," I say, suddenly inserting myself into the situation, "but who the fuck are you?" My head feels hot with wine as I stand up from my chair, not thinking about percentages or predictive models based on likely hardscrabble upbringings and forearm mass index.

"Chuck, don't!" says Beth.

And that's when the lights go out.

19

I'd never really considered getting injured.

I've thought about getting shot a hundred different ways, but in each instance, I die.

Except now it has me wondering. What if I charge out into the quad or mail sorting room or navy yard and get winged instead? I could try to get back up for another go, but the gunman might already have moved on by that point, or my leg's broken, or my arm no longer works right.

As I press a towel full of ice against my new black eye, I wonder why I've never thought of this. This not being killed instantly. I have to be sure or none of this will matter.

At least for me.

In other words, I have to make sure he doesn't miss.

—

Of course, Chuck didn't miss my left eye last night. So here I am, watching the trees gently bend outside the window, trying not to squint.

I have no idea how I got back to my room.

I remember Beth helping me up in the restaurant followed by me throwing up in some bushes, but that's about it.

Did I let myself in? Did she?

I woke up still wearing my clothes, so there's that.

—

Lots of people have gotten punched or worse in the pursuit of mathematics.

Turing was castrated.

Rhazes was beaten over the head with one of his own books, which introduced Hippocrates to the Muslim world, and which also caused him to go blind.

—

The reverse happened to an alcoholic futon salesman in Alaska. He was beaten to within an inch of his life and discovered soon after he suddenly could perfectly recreate complex fractals by hand, not to mention describe the discrete structure of space-time based on Planck length and quantum black holes.

—

I have yet to visit Alaska on one of my trips.

They only rarely have mass shootings, which is interesting when you consider they are number one when it comes to gun ownership per capita.

In fact, over 60% of their residents own guns.

They shoot at bears like we swat flies.

Children probably shoot their way out of breakfast and take target practice at recess.

Only North Dakota, New Hampshire, and Hawaii have had zero mass shootings since 2013. God knows what those places have in common.

The state I've been to most is Florida, in fact.

I feel sorry for Florida. It looks like when a dream breaks down, but you remember it was a wonderful dream that will never be repeated in quite the same way.

One of my favorite motels is in Florida, too. The Aqua View. It has a pineapple shaped pool and the rooms have bamboo accents like Lauren Bacall is going to walk out of the wallpaper.

Last I was there someone tried to kill off most of a DMV, but I had the day wrong.

—

He drove a Prius.

He smiled when posing for pictures at all-American barbecues.

He used a sawed-off shotgun.

—

No motel franchises for me. They lack a certain humanity. Just like with train travel, there's a hint of romance that still lurks in old motels. It's in the neon. It's in the rugs and the wallpaper.

—

No one thinks of Florida when they think of math.

They think of China. They think of Germany.

When I think of Florida, I think of Gatorade and the fact that it's illegal to sing while wearing swimwear in public.

That's true, actually.

—

I do suddenly remember Beth saying something about a restraining order she had against Chuck. A hundred feet, I think. Or was it 100 yards? In any case, she'd left him and I think she and Henry have been hiding out in the motel until they can make their next move.

This is all me just me hypothesizing, of course.

I mean, obviously, there are some facts like the existence of Chuck and my black eye and the restraining order, but I don't know anything for certain.

Sort of like the Method.

There are hard ratios and percentages, but there are also hunches and foreboding vibes that lurk beyond verifiable truth.

—

One thing about last night that makes me happy:

I didn't freeze in the face of Chuck, which is good to know going forward. There will be no time to freeze at the Trigger Event.

—

The second thing about last night that makes me happy:

Apparently, I did some noodling on the Method before I'd gone to bed. Under a half-empty pitcher of Harvey Wallbangers, I found a solution that confirms the date and the town, but also three names which weren't there before:

Spencer Geddes.

Lucinda Flowers.

Manny Alocer.

—

As this is the first time the Method has given me actual names, I decide to celebrate with a fresh round of Wallbangers. When I open the door to get more ice down the hall a folded piece of paper falls to the floor.

I pick it up and unfold it.

I'm sorry, it says. *I hope you feel better. I think it's best we probably don't see each other right now. Between Chuck and my son and just trying to make ends meet…it's just a lot. I wish things were different, but they just aren't. I hope you understand.*

No "XOXO" or "thinking of you madly."

Just "Beth."

—

Part of me is upset at how things ended, but another part of me is relieved to refocus my attention on the matter at hand.

Especially with this new information.

It's easier to lose focus than one would think doing this sort of business. For one, there's a lot of monotony in what I do.

Freeways tend to blend together when you're driving at night. You can only just make out the edges of hills. Blobs of forest beyond the light poles.

The motels, like I said, are usually of a type, which again is something I find immensely satisfying, but still their surroundings can dull the senses.

The diners. The pharmacies.

For all the differences in this country, there's an underlying sameness that only the constant traveler can't help but notice. I'm talking about truckers. Serial killers. Math hobbyists.

In any case, I tend to stay away from relationships because what I do is tricky to explain. Plus, I'm usually not around more than a day or two.

Being a loner in your smaller towns has its challenges, but for the most part I've steered clear of any new relationships.

I have the Method.

I have Zoe's incessant calling.

I have the memory of Marion leaning over the steam of a freshly opened dishwasher after just telling me about getting drilled by the number-two realtor in our zip code.

—

I have the memory of the green sweater, too.

I remember what her neck looked like.

I remember the Mountain Dew logo glowing, almost floating just above her right ear like a satellite orbiting the saddest thing ever.

—

I walk down the open-air hallway to the ice machine near the stairs. About a dozen domelets of ice clank home in my little bucket like snowy jewels.

As I head back to my room, I see Henry walking towards the pool.

I yell down to him, "Good morning, Henry."

He looks up, but doesn't say anything. After opening the gated entrance to the pool, he lays out a small arsenal of water guns then turns his back to me.

I mock-laugh like I'm in on the joke, but still nothing.

—

Settling in with the fresh ice. Thinking about a new cocktail. Thinking about the names. Thinking about why there are three of them instead of just one.

That's when there's a knock at the door.

Beth?

Coming to check on my eye?

Yes.

Coming to say she was wrong about the whole thing. Coming to say we should go out again or just have drinks in my room and order Chinese and massage each other using organic, sage-infused oils.

"Just a sec," I say through the door.

A quick look in the mirror to straighten my hair.

Tidy the bed.

When I open the door, I find Zoe looking back at me as if I were the creature from the black lagoon.

"Dad, what in the fuck is going on?"

"Hey, Blueberry," I say.

20

Here now is my only daughter, sitting at the end of my motel bed. The beautiful Swiss-watch precision of everything violently whiplashed into the Iowa sun.

She's sitting with her arms crossed, looking at me with her mother's disbelieving eyes. She asks me, "Why do you have a black eye?"

"Well, it's hard to explain," I tell her.

"Try."

"Chuck. That's Beth's ex-husband. He punched me. Or, at least, soon-to-be ex. Do you want a drink?"

"It's ten-thirty in the morning."

"Of course. What was I thinking?"

She looks around the room and sighs like she did when she was little and couldn't figure out a math problem.

"Okay, what are you making?" she asks, defeated.

—

Zoe's a journalist, but she's just starting out.

"That's probably how you found me," I say proudly, raising my Harvey Wallbanger and taking a sip.

"I'm a fact-checker," she says with her mother's eyeroll.

"But you went to journalism school. You just have to put your time in. You'll have your own byline lickety-split."

"Dad, it's really competitive."

"I'm sure, but if you just—"

"*Dad.*"

"Okay, okay. How did you find me anyway?"

"A fact-checker never tells."

—

So much of having a grown kid is not getting to talk about the past.

You want to talk about Thanksgiving from '99?

Forget it.

You want to talk about Crater Lake and how Marion twisted her ankle at the Cleetwood Cove Trail parking lot because she'd had too much to drink?

Go to hell.

The dark-blue Chevy Blazer that no matter what always smelled like wet dog and bananas?

Fuck off!

—

At the Middle Eastern deli, eating salads peppered with rubbery chicken, she says, "Mom isn't herself."

Somehow, I don't throw my salad at the window or try to light myself on fire in a one-man Viking funeral.

"What's wrong with her?" I ask, using the noncommittal expression of an anesthetized scallop.

"I just don't think she thought she was this person, you know? Like that she was capable of doing this."

"Doing what?"

"Blowing up a family."

Zoe is always the thoughtful family historian in all of this. Seeing all the different angles and points of view. I was always caught up in the moment, in the details. It's important to look at the big picture. I love that about Zoe, but it also makes me sad for her.

Was she the only one who was still actively trying?

Was she the last real Prumont?

—

Zoe wants everything to go back to summer barbecues and Christmas morning.

But that's the difference between a twenty-two-year-old fresh out of college and a middle-aged, black-eyed ex-healthcare executive who's drinking Harvey Wallbangers at ten-thirty in the morning while attempting to predict the next Columbine.

—

What does Poisson think?

The engineer should receive a complete mathematical education, but for what should it serve him? To see the different aspects of things and to see them quickly; he has no time to hunt mice.

—

What does Klebold say?

I'm full of love and nobody wants it.

—

She gets the room next to mine.

"I took a couple days off and I'm convincing you to come home," she tells me happily, but I can tell this is a sort of mission for her that comes with heavier implications.

I help with her bag and put it on the bed. She has the same big window looking out on the same big trees softly bending.

"I get that you needed to get away from everything back home, but why are you here?" she asks, gesturing out the door. "Why are you in fucking Iowa?"

"That's hard to explain," I say. "But it's nice, don't you think?"

"Dad, remember this is my job."

"What's that supposed to mean?"

"It means I find facts."

21

I'm now standing behind a telephone pole so that Manny Alocer doesn't see me, wondering if I should pretend to be something other than a stalker.

I could be someone looking for their cat.

I could be insane and huffing gasoline.

Those are things people do behind telephone poles.

—

Kurt Gödel thought everyone was trying to poison him.

Paul Erdős randomly showed up at people's houses to work out math problems.

—

To be honest, I'm really just winging it.

Unlike regional healthcare marketing, there's no precedent for whatever this is. Other than some understanding of math, it really is an exercise of imagination. I always had a good imagination, my career choice and love for Saabs notwithstanding.

I used to have all sorts of ideas.

I wanted to live abroad for a year. In Luxembourg or Helsinki. I wanted to cook a goose for Christmas. I wanted to have an extramarital affair with a woman named Belinda.

I did have an affair with Alise, however.

That's part of what made it hard to distill everything post-Real Deal.

How could I be mad?

Except I knew my fling really had meant nothing. If you could even call it a fling. It was really just a mash of lips and taut khakis in the back seat of a cab. Did she try to unzip my pants? I think she only wanted me to think she tried.

She did lick my throat.

Of course, we'd talked a lot before then.

We let our knees touch at lunch, and one time on the office booze cruise, she let me see her underwear, which had purple polka dots.

That was before it became impossible to hold back for one-and-a-half minutes in a dusty yellow Ford Caprice.

—

I would never tell Zoe this.

Dr. Killjoy and the secret London club would be erased forever.

I would lose all leverage. It's an extremely fluid and complex situation. Victimhood has gradients. It's never black-and-white.

—

Speaking of white, Manny is not. That's a concern. Sixty-four percent of mass shooters since 1982 are white. Only ten percent Latino.

I pretend to get a phone call and walk back to my car. I'm looking for anything that makes me look official in some way. I find a clipboard in the back seat. That'll do.

As I walk back to Manny's house, I can hear someone playing Van Morrison's "Sweet Thing." It's coming from a house overlooking a broken down truck in a field. The song just sort of floats there in the blue spring Iowa air like a black-throated warbler.

—

Zoe had another Van Morrison song she always listened to on the record player I bought her for her ninth birthday. "Into the Mystic."

Or was it "Astral Weeks"?

It was always that or the Beatles, in any case. I tried to get her into Aretha Franklin, but it didn't take for one reason or another. I pushed too early perhaps. And I don't think it was one of her better albums.

Zoe is not here, of course.

I had to leave the motel early before she woke up.

My phone is already buzzing in my coat pocket with missed calls and texts.

—

A boy wearing a Batman mask answers the door.

"Hello," I say. "Is your dad home?"

"Fuck that," says Batman, giggling as he runs off somewhere.

"Can I help you?"

I turn around, startled.

"Sorry, I was working in the garage," says a stout man wearing a paint-spattered tangerine polo and a Hawkeyes ball cap.

"Oh, sure thing," I say, only realizing now for some reason that I might literally be face to face with a future mass murderer. "Don't want to bother you, but I'm starting a neighborhood watch and, well, I just wanted to introduce myself to the block. I'm Bill," I say, surprising myself a little at the bland choice for a name. Why not Arlen or Octavius? But then again, Octavius might be a stretch for the block captain of a neighborhood watch in Little Lake, Iowa.

"Nice to meet you. I'm Manny," says the potential mass murderer.

We shake hands.

"How long have you lived here?" I ask.

"Oh, maybe five years. Are you new here?"

"Yes, I'm just a couple blocks that way," I say, pointing vaguely in another direction.

"The brick house on the corner that just sold?"

"Yep."

"Welcome to the neighborhood."

"Thanks. How many in the family?"

"Just the little guy with the mouth you already met. And my wife."

I write something down on my clipboard.

"Great," I tell him. "Just trying to get an idea of who belongs to who. You know how these things are. Everything helps. By the way, they make me ask, but are there any guns in the home?"

"Guns? I have my hunting rifle. Who makes you ask?"

"The national charter for the, uh, Neighborhood Safety Federation. If I do certain things, our watch could qualify for special grants and even scholarships in conflict management."

"I see. Do you have a card or anything?"

"You know, I'm fresh out, but I'll be down around this way tomorrow. Should I stick one in your mailbox?"

—

I drive home feeling like a jackass. My job is to analyze and observe. Where do I get off pretending to be Bill, the Neighborhood Safety Federation lackey? And what if Manny really is the person who guns down a bunch of innocent people in a few days? What would've stopped him from starting the festivities a little early or just getting some practice in before the big day?

I suppose I do know he's a gun owner now, so there's that.

Although I probably could've figured that out with a phone call from the safety of my motel room, enjoying a Wallbanger.

This is the problem with the incompleteness of the Method. It's hard to know exactly how far I need to go to make up for whatever is missing in the numbers. The difference is I'm not used to getting names like this. I'm typically only staking out certain cities and towns, and within those areas, looking at probable hot spots, then groups of people, races, genders, unemployed vs. employed. This feels different. This feels like Jim Rockford meets Georg Cantor.

Who the fuck do I think I am?

—

THE PRUMONT METHOD

Sometimes, the Method makes no sense.

Sometimes, the Method is like a broken-down truck in a field.

22

The Method can be scary when it's right.

Like in Buffalo.

That's where I saw a shooter for the first time before it happened.

At least, I think I did.

In the days leading up to it, he would get coffee where I got coffee.

It was a little campus bistro. Euro Café it was called. The coffee wasn't any good, but it was cheap. The chairs and tables outside looked out on a pretty little canal with tall Greek-looking pillars along the edge, signifying something or another.

I'm pretty sure he was the one wearing the red windbreaker.

The shooter, that is.

He had long black hair with a mint-green bandana over his ears. He always got there before I did and drank his coffee alone, looking at his phone. He didn't look like someone who was going to stack bodies behind a refreshment counter.

But who does?

In any case, I didn't realize it was him until it was too late, which is to say after the soda fountain and walking down the street covered in blood, making the children stare.

I mean, if it was him.

I suppose it could just as easily have been some campus agitator or Antifa recruiter.

Then again, what would I have done if I knew without exception that it was him?

Would I have gone ahead with my plan or would I have tried to stop him?

That would probably be the less selfish thing to do. But you never know. He could've been armed each of those mornings. He could've had all manner of weapon concealed under his windbreaker. He could've shot that girl with the golden retriever right behind me. He could've shot those teenagers in muddy soccer uniforms getting croissants. He could've lost his fucking mind.

Except, hadn't he already?

—

I always wonder about this. When does it dawn on them? Are they scrambling eggs or doing laundry one day? Then, suddenly, gunshots and screaming? And necks bent unnaturally? When does it come into their head?

In any case, trying to stop a maniac like that could've ended just as badly or worse.

Better yet, I could've made an anonymous call to the police.

They would've found the AR-15 and the sawed-off shotgun in his van. They would've found the manifesto on "racial and cultural purity," among other nonsense.

But what about my obituary?

What about the doctors?

Zoe's reconfigured future recollection of who her dad really was?

Then again, who knows if that was him?

The shooter I mean. The one in the red windbreaker.

You never know.

—

Although, looking at the pictures in the paper the next day, I think it had to be. And if that's the case, I even saw him on the morning of the actual day.

Only hours to go at that point. It was a Thursday, if I remember correctly. I could've spoken to him. I could've walked right up to him and asked for the time or to pass me the creamer. What do you say to a person like that?

What's your motive?

Name three famous dead people you most want to have dinner with?

—

Although, typically, most shooters aren't that interesting.

They have anger by the boatload, but not much insight. People always feel cheated when these guys blow their brains out instead of going on the stand, but I think people by and large would only be disappointed. Very few, in fact, realize just how dull these lunatics really are.

Manifestoes are fucking boring.

Diaries are self-absorbed.

But still. I could've walked up to him and popped a question all the same. Or at least found out what he liked in his coffee.

Did he see me? I wonder. All those mornings? Possibly, although I imagine his mind was elsewhere.

Regardless, I think the numbers put me in close proximity to him even without giving me his name.

The Method is subtle. It's elegant, really. Maybe even magical.

I just need to remember to tune in better. I have to let the game come to me. Like all those basketball announcers. They always talk about the star player who's pushing to do too much. It could be over-dribbling or taking one too many contested threes. The idea being that if you let "it" come to you, everything will fall into place naturally. Essentially, that's what math is.

Things just click.

23

Zoe has deli sandwiches and two bottles of beer.

"We going on a picnic?" I ask.

"Yeah, in your room."

She's clever. Using a gentler tactic to woo me home. To pretend death doesn't exist. To pretend the Real Deal never smacked my wife's backside in the shower like she was Trigger.

To make everything magically go back to the way it was.

—

We sit on the edge of my bed like the White Cliffs of Dover. The parking lot is our English Channel. The crows our gulls.

"This is nice," she says as I wonder what's coming next.

—

Watching her unwrap the sandwiches, I can see Marion. Her carefulness. Or rather, her attention to detail. She's nothing like her mother overall, but resembles her in so many little terrifying ways.

—

You know what Poisson said about successful marriages and mathematical probability?

Nothing.

Not on record at least.

Some people say things, but honestly, nobody really fucking knows.

—

Zoe is eating her turkey and cheddar on sourdough like she's with a special delegation from the State Department.

"So, how have you been?"

"I'm fine," I say, snapping off a beer cap at the makeshift bar.

"That looks like a lot of booze," she says, eyeing the bottles crowding under the wall-mounted TV.

"Well, it travels with me so I save money, you know."

As I say this, I know how dumb it sounds, but it's also not worth the discussion. And anyway, it only seems like more than usual. When you have a bar at home, it just sits there in a darkened cabinet. No doubt it looks gratuitous on a countertop like this. Hell, I would think the same thing.

"Where have you been?" she asks.

"Here and some other places."

"What other places?"

"Los Angeles, New Orleans, Minnesota, all over the Midwest…"

"Wow. You seeing old friends?"

"Not really."

"I have a boyfriend, by the way."

She says this as she gets off the bed. She's never been serious about anyone to make a statement like that. Deploying a new tactic?

"That's great," I say. "Who is the lucky guy?"

"He's in advertising. Sort of like you."

—

A lot of my friends have sons-in-law now. Everybody younger than me feels like a child. Since when did high schoolers look like ten-year-olds? I'm not sure how to think about it, except that it's inevitable, like glacial drift or wearing sweats on Sunday meant for a much larger, even more depressed person than yourself.

—

Who is Spencer Geddes?

Who is Lucinda Bates?

Why am I in an Iowa motel room eating turkey sandwiches with my daughter?

The clock is ticking.

—

"Dad."

"What?"

"What in the hell is this?"

"What in the hell is what?"

"On the wall."

I'm so used to it, I don't even notice that she's pointing to all the papers covered in numbers taped up on the wall. She looks at me like she is concerned. She looks at me like I'm starring in a movie about someone who is absolutely going to be stowed in a nuthouse by the end of it.

"Oh that?" I say.

"Yes, that."

—

When she first started to walk, she would scream as she waddled down the hall.

"Ahhhhhhhhhhhh!"

So many times I would put a bowl of broccoli in front of her and she would look at me as if I'd just car-bombed Bert and Ernie.

—

I tell her everything except the part about Buffalo. I'm still not sure I've processed that one yet. Yes, she'll think I'm crazy, but not crazy enough to call the police. I think.

"So, you're just like some mathematical genius all of a sudden?" she asks, taking it all very well it seems.

"No. I'm just good with numbers and I got lucky."

"Have you at all entertained the notion that this Theory or whatever you call it is all bullshit? I mean, last year alone there were what, 300 mass shootings?"

"417 actually."

"Well, great. That's more than one a day, Dad. Even if it's incredibly remote, what are the chances this *theory* of yours is completely random luck and you're getting close or not so close based on the fact that there are so fucking many of these things?"

"So, you think even the things I've gotten right have been all luck?"

"Yes, because there's no fucking way this is real."

"Have you always been swearing this much?"

"Holy fucking Christ."

"Listen, let's calm down and have a drink."

"No. And what's with all the drinks all the time? Are you like living in a Dashiell Hammett novel all of a sudden?"

"I know it seems crazy, but I don't know how to explain it."

"And these three guys, you're just going to follow them around until one of them starts shooting up the town? That's your plan?"

"Two guys. One female."

"Holy fucking Christ."

"Blueberry, will you please just sit down?"

"What would Mom say about all this?"

"Marion? What does she have to do with any of this?"

"Well, oh, I don't know, she's your wife?"

"Okay, can we lose the tone?"

"What if I told her about all this?"

"You won't tell her."

"Why the fuck not?"

"Because if you tell her, you know it's over between her and I for good. You can have Thanksgiving with the Real Deal every year and kiss my ass goodbye. That's why the fuck not."

—

Sometimes, I'm unsure about everything. My life. The Method.

I'm certain Poisson had times where he wasn't sure about the particle theory of light or the calculus of variations.

As I think about this, I can hear my daughter next door throwing pillows against the wall.

I'm glad she's here, actually, even though she poses a threat to my mission.

In any case, everything's been moving so fast lately I'd forgotten I would've never seen her again had she not found me.

How could I forget that I wonder?

Am I taking this seriously enough?

Being a father?

24

What would other people think about the Method? If they'd somehow devised the same equation, what would they do? This is something I often wonder about.

Of course, context is everything. How did they feel about their life pre-Method? Were they happy? Were they civically-minded? Or were they somewhat self-centered ex-regional healthcare marketing execs whose wife's buttocks have known the trembling sting of the Real Deal?

I've barreled ahead due to my own circumstances, but that doesn't mean I haven't thought about this from other angles and points of view. I could see how someone might see this as black and white. I could see how someone might think I'm jeopardizing the lives of others for my own personal gain. Except, one has to take into account that the whole thing is just so jumbo-size crazy, not to mention tragic, that it's difficult to nail down at any one time the moral topography of it all.

I will be saving someone's life. So, there's that. That's not a small thing. Maybe multiple people's lives. Maybe an important politician or a sick child. Maybe both.

I will get there before he kills anyone. That's the whole point of this, obviously. The stars just haven't aligned yet. Everything has to be perfect. If I'd told the cops in Spokane or Corpus Christi, they would've thought I was crazy.

Although Buffalo was different.

If I'd told them in Buffalo, maybe the neck of the girl in the green sweater would have looked normal. Maybe she'd be living in Asunción now or falling in love with an obscure poet. Maybe she wouldn't have been stacked beneath a soda fountain like one of those sepia-toned cadaver-heaps from Chancellorsville.

—

I've only told two other people about the Method, but they were random strangers.

I told one on purpose, the other was by mistake.

—

Intentionally, I passed along my discovery to a well-known math professor at Princeton. Just to get his opinion. But he never responded.

Of course, mathematicians are famously competitive, and that was the nascent stages of the Method, so maybe it wasn't as accessible yet. I'm sure if he saw it now, he would likely have something to say. Not that it really matters at this point.

—

The other person I told was at a bar across the street from my motel in Corpus Christi. The Cactus Inn, as a matter of fact. In any case, I was drunk as a skunk, which is such a phenomenal phrase because nothing else quite captures that heightened state of intoxication. It was right after finding out the shooting was actually a day earlier in

Grand Junction. Even though it was early in the Method's evolution, I was still quite upset.

In any case, I had a few too many mezcal Manhattans and started talking to a truck driver from Barstow. When he asked what I did, I told him I was close to completing a mathematical thingamajig that could predict where the next mass shooting would take place. He laughed at first, but then he could see I was serious.

"Why would you do that?" he asked.

"What do you mean?" I said, wondering if he was drunker than he'd let on.

"You're talking about predicting the future."

"So?"

"So, where's the fun in that?"

—

Mezcal Manhattan:

2 ounces mezcal

1 ounce sweet vermouth

2 dashes bitters

Maraschino cherry and/or orange twist

—

I almost told my high school math teacher. But why? What could he possibly say? And he had to be almost ninety if he was even still alive. Who cares at that point? I know I wouldn't.

—

At some point, I simply started asking people wherever the numbers took me, "If you could predict one thing in the future, what would it be?"

Unsurprisingly, most people say the stock market or football scores.

A woman in Boise gave my favorite response: "I want to see where my third marriage goes."

—

Math has a sense of humor.

In France, a pie chart is sometimes referred to as a "camembert."

Not laugh-out-loud, but "math-funny" anyway.

—

Did you hear the one about the statistician?

Probably.

Or

Why was the fraction apprehensive about marrying the decimal?

Because he would have to convert.

—

I didn't tell Zoe everything, of course. I didn't tell her about the trying to get myself killed part. Or the part about the doctors. Or the part about the girl in the green sweater.

—

I guess there are some things a daughter can never really know about her father.

Like large swaths of one's college years, or how you almost drove into a light pole that one night.

But I couldn't lie to Zoe. Not that I don't mind bending the truth now and again. It's just that she would sniff out a lie from me in a second. Her eyes go right through me like serrated Gerbers.

I'm really not even that good at lying, or for that matter, even spotting liars.

Hence the Real Deal.

Hence all the bullshit I feasted on during time served in regional healthcare marketing.

That said, it doesn't really matter at this point. There's not much that can get in my way if you think about it. Other than a bullet or two.

25

For some reason, I answer my phone without looking at who's calling, which is something I never do.

It's Marion.

"Sorry," she says. "I got the number from Zoe. She says you get new burner phones all the time or whatever, but I thought I'd try."

I don't respond. Instead, I try to gather myself as if I'd just been T-boned at an intersection by a two-story float in the middle of Mardi Gras.

"Listen, Rog," she continues, headlong. "I know you hate me right now, and I get it, I totally get it. But I was hoping maybe we could try to, I don't know, talk about it at least. Can we try that?"

Why didn't I just fuck that Alise? I could've just insisted we get a room or something instead of just laughing it off awkwardly. We could've made elaborate pillow forts every week for the last three years and role-played in the shower. I could've been Poisson and she could've been Sophie Germain, who actually studied under Gauss. In any case, then I could've just laughed in Marion's face the way one laughs when one no longer gives a shit.

"Rog, can we at least talk?"

"Marion?" I say.

"Yes?"

"Please don't call me anymore."

"But Ro—"

26

I predicted something once before.

When I was younger, I foresaw that I would not be able to make it as an adult, except at some point, I started lying to myself. The future became incredibly bright and without shape. Hope is shapeless, but at the same time, it has the ability to cut to the bone.

I remember watching my dad go to work and making phone calls with business associates in the kitchen after dinner, and I knew it couldn't be done. Not replicated in any way whatsoever.

He was like Everest or Leonhard Euler.

Or whoever invented the banana split.

Some people have what it takes and some don't. I've only pretended that I could do it, but everyone has to at least try, don't they?

Look at Updike. Look at Koons.

My hopes and dreams are on life support.

My organs are made of bottle-green glass.

27

I drive all around Little Lake. I drive past the high school and the police department and the Walmart.

Will this person be shot?

Or maybe this one?

—

Most of them burn ants when they're kids, probably. They burn them by the millions. They watch the burning ants, almost expressionless.

They're like Hitler to ants. They're like Pol Pot.

How did the 20th Century produce so many great mathematicians and so many genocidists at the same time?

—

Math has been around since murder.

Markings on animal bones indicate that humans have been doing math since around 30,000 B.C.

Cain didn't shank Abel with part of a plough until 3905 B.C.

People say prostitution is the oldest profession, but it's actually math.

—

Math is the Final Solution.

Math is the Electoral College.

—

When I return to the motel, I find Zoe waiting outside my door.

"I'm going to help you," she says. "And then you'll come home. That's the deal."

"Deal," I say, knowing it's the only way to make her stop. Plus, I'll be able to spend quality time with her before this all comes to an end.

We order pizza and I walk her through the Method again. I can tell she's not quite sure if she believes any of it, but she will humor me to make everything go back to the way it was.

We are in the same room, and yet, we are in two different worlds.

"Since when were you this math person?" she asks, sighing and puffing out her cheeks as she looks up at the number-filled pages on the wall.

"I always liked math," I say, straining a Bee's Knees into a champagne coupe. "It's just something I sort of gave up on until recently."

"But is this normal? To write equations on the wall and drive from town to town, hunting down mass killers from the future?"

"Well, not when you put it like that."

"So why didn't you become an engineer or something? Why the fuck healthcare marketing?"

I tell her I didn't major in mathematics or anything. I just did it on the side.

"In fact, I didn't really know what I wanted to do," I say.

—

Oliver Heaviside was self-taught and he predicted the existence of the ionosphere.

Benjamin Banneker had little formal education and predicted the solar eclipse that occurred on April 14th, 1789.

—

"I've never done anything like this," I explain. "I'm as surprised as you are. And as far as healthcare marketing, your guess is as good as mine. It just seemed like something to do. Life always seemed that way to me. Just something to pass the time. This is the first time I've ever felt like I'm actually doing something."

"Yeah," says Zoe, "but what exactly is it you're doing?"

Bee's Knees

2 ounces gin

½ ounce fresh lemon juice

¾ ounce honey

28

I am a selfish person. Everybody is selfish to a degree, but I have to be in the 90th percentile. Or at least very close. My father and my father's father were selfish men. The only person that makes me realize this is Zoe. With Marion and the others, it never bothered me at the end of the day. But Zoe's different. She makes me want to be better, which is maybe one of the main points of children after all.

—

"That's life, baby," is something Zoe used to say when she was three or four. I would ask Marion if we were out of cocktail peanuts, and Zoe, standing in the middle of the kitchen, would cross her arms over her bare chest and casually declare, "That's life, baby."

How had I not said goodbye to her properly? Was I really just going to leave her behind like that? Just walk into a hail of bullets without hugging my little girl one last time?

The thing is, Zoe would probably understand what I was doing if she wasn't emotionally attached to the situation. If I wasn't her dad.

She has that in her DNA.

That repulsion to failure.

—

I hand her a Bee's Knees and she turns the glass carefully in her hands, examining it like it might tell her the future or produce some kind of genie.

Then she takes a deep breath.

"You say you've gotten close. Like how close?"

"Very close."

"You're not going to tell me, are you?"

She looks at me with a mix of love and bafflement.

29

I often can't sleep. Especially lately. In the middle of the night, I'll open the curtains and look out at the trees, or I'll noodle on some numbers, or see if there aren't some basketball highlights on TV to fall asleep to.

I think part of the reason is the fact that the Trigger Event is so close now, which means the end is close. I've been thinking so much about the Method and the potential shooter and Zoe that I haven't really given much consideration to the afterlife. Not that I believe in God or anything, but I don't like going into things unprepared.

It's probably just uncharged blackness or nothingness, but I suppose it could be something else altogether.

Maybe consciousness retreats into a recurring dream.

Maybe it's a mixtape of Vivaldi and the Kinks with Venus in the background epically crashing into Deimos.

—

Gauss believed in the afterlife. He thought life without some form of immortality to be absurd.

Turing and Lobachevsky were outright atheists.

I'm not sure what Whitman thought about God.

—

I must always be thinking about death on some level.

My new vocation or mission or whatever you want to call it virtually surrounds me with death. Or literally, in the case of the soda fountain in Buffalo. And now, with my time winding down and Zoe here, it all seems very real in a way that it maybe didn't before.

Buffalo made things real.

But it all happened so fast and I wasn't quite sure then about the Method in the way that I am now.

I'll miss the motels and the driving at night and everyday feeling further and further away from whoever I used to be.

—

I turn on the TV. Looking out the window just now, I know there are killers everywhere. My killer is out there. There are killers driving up and down the highway. There are killers in other motels. Killers thick in the night like fireflies.

—

When I go outside for ice to help make something that will put me back to sleep, I am surprised to see Beth swimming in the pool. I am even more surprised to see that she's naked. I freeze in the shadows and watch her. Her buttocks glowing wintergreen in the moonlight shot through bending trees. She looks very graceful with her hair up. She is a proud skinny dipper who wants to bring happiness to the world. For a moment, I stand frozen. Her pendulous breasts sluicing the purple chlorinated depths. Her muff acting as a fuzzy rudder. I fantasize about fixing a nice refreshing drink for her while she breaststrokes around the deep end. Watch her boldly climb the ladder, baring her big cold breasts followed by the snow driven swoop of her ass. I almost call down to her. But then I think better of it.

The ice machine will make that whirring noise, too, so I decide against the whole affair and turn back.

"Scotch doesn't need ice," I say to the scotch.

30

I thought when this all started it would be a solitary act, like becoming a monk or being exiled to Elba, but it's been nice having Zoe around. Even if she is nosy and doesn't really believe in the Method. Or that I'm not lost without Marion.

She knocks on my door around eight with coffees the size of desk lamps.

"So, who are these guys?" she asks, handing me one of the steaming, lamp-size Americanos.

"What guys?"

"The names or whatever. The names from your math thingy."

I tell her the names, holding my tongue on the "thingy" remark.

"So, your equation or whatever has narrowed down thousands of people to these two guys and a woman."

"Yeah."

"So, who is it?"

"Possibly Geddes. Who knows?"

"Why Geddes?"

"Most shooters are white males. Manny does own a gun, however."

"And you know that how?"

"Because he told me."

"You talked to him? In fucking person?"

"Yeah."

"You just walked up to this potential mass shooter and said, 'Hey, do you have any guns around?'"

"No, I pretended I was starting a neighborhood watch and needed to get basic security type information."

"Holy shit, Dad."

"Smart, huh?"

"Jesus. You really think you are in a Dashiell Hammett novel, don't you?"

—

We are driving to the county courthouse to do some sleuthing.

"You think the woman can't do it?" Zoe asks, looking out the window at the passing lake, which will be where they launch the floating water lanterns to honor all the victims.

"What woman?"

"Lucinda. You don't think she has what it takes to lose her mind?"

"There have only been three lady shooters since 1982."

"Lady shooters?"

"Female. Sorry, Blueberry"

"But she could do it. She could lose her fucking mind just like any man."

I see where this is going. I say, "I think women typically tend to focus their anger on the source rather than take it out on a bunch of strangers."

"Well, duh, men are idiots."

"What about this new boyfriend of yours?" I say, changing the subject.

"Ha! That mercenary prima donna?"

—

When Zoe was in fourth grade, a boy named Garreth had a crush on her. He kept asking to sit next to her at lunch.

"Boys are so pathetic," she told me one day after school. "But at least they don't talk too much."

I didn't disagree.

—

Zoe tells me to wait by the entrance of the courthouse while she goes to the records room.

I see a deputy manning the metal detector staring dumbly into the middle distance.

"Excuse me," I say passing the time. "Just curious if you had any idea what the biggest crime ever was around here."

"I wouldn't know that, sir," he says as if he has known no joy in life.

"A man killed his whole family with a knife a few years back," says someone to my left.

I look over and see what looks like a homeless person. He's wearing an old letterman's jacket and sipping something hot from one of those retro plaid thermoses you find in 99 cent stores.

"It was Christmas Day," he continues, not looking up from his thermos. "He stabbed his mother-in-law, his wife, and his two kids with a big hunting knife. He skinned the mother-in-law in the bathtub and then he burnt down their Christmas tree. Then he just walked down to the local police station and told them, 'I did it, motherfuckers.'"

"Jesus," I say.

"Yep. He told the cop he didn't want to celebrate no Christmas that year, but they wouldn't listen. He also said the turkey was overcooked. You believe that shit?"

I shake my head in disbelief, for a moment wondering if it was him.

—

In 1949, in Camden, New Jersey, Howard Unruh walked around his neighborhood for twelve minutes killing thirteen people and injuring three.

During the ensuing shootout with police from his home, an enterprising reporter found his number in the phone book and just called him up.

Reporter: Is this Howard?
Howard: Yes...what's the last name of the party you want?
Reporter: Unruh.
Howard: What's the last name of the party you want?
Reporter: Unruh. I'm a friend, and I want to know what they're doing to you.

Howard: They're not doing a damned thing to me, but I'm doing plenty to them.
Reporter: How many have you killed?
Howard: I don't know yet, because I haven't counted them...but it looks like a pretty good score.
Reporter: Why are you killing people?
Howard: I don't know. I can't answer that yet, I'm too busy. [loud gunfire] I'll have to talk to you later...a couple of friends are coming to get me...

—

During his "Walk of Death," Unruh killed Maurice and Rose Cohen in their apartment, but their son Charles survived by hiding in a closet.

Interesting fact: Charles Cohen's granddaughter was a survivor of the Parkland shootings sixty-nine years later.

She hid, too.

Her heart was a hummingbird that day.

Just like her grandfather's on a Friday in 1949. His heart couldn't beat fast enough as he heard Unruh shoot his mother, who was hiding in a different closet.

Or trying to, anyway.

—

"Hide, Charles, hide!" Charles' mother said lastly.

—

"Let's go," Zoe says, skipping down the worn marble steps.

I ask her what she found out.

"Manny seems on the up-and-up, but this Geddes character, he's worth looking into. He's got a couple priors, nothing big, but one was an aggravated misdemeanor for open carry without a permit."

"What about Lucinda?"

"Oh yeah, that was a weird one."

"Weird how?"

"Well, for one, she's nine years old."

31

Who goes on a stakeout with their daughter?

Who obsesses over someone named Kevin the Real Deal?

—

"Regional healthcare marketing," said zero famous poets, mathematicians, or maritime explorers ever.

—

When I walked off the plane in Buffalo, a voice in my head told me I should leave, but I kept moving forward for some reason.

My brain was so attuned with the numbers it was like seeing the future.

Like a premonition?

Like everyone who second-guessed jumping out of a trench in Ypres or Dinant, then did it anyway?

—

Lots of famous people died while staying in motels:

Martin Luther King stayed in room 306.

Sam Cooke was in room 12.

Marion Crane was in room 1.

—

The first motel we stayed in as a family was not far from Point Reyes Beach. Marion (my Marion, not Alfred Hitchcock's) was setting the table and I opened another bottle of Burgundy. There were no clouds for the first time all weekend.

Zoe, in just her underwear, kept picking up my duffel bag and then pretending to go off to work.

She'd wave goodbye and say, "Gah, go!"

She did it over and over for at least thirty minutes until she finally went back to inspect her cold cheeseburger like she had been dispatched from the NTSB.

—

When Zoe was nine years old, she was acting like a seventeen-year-old. There's certainly the possibility of an ex-husband or two in her future.

"Divorce isn't failure," Marion will tell her.

Or if she doesn't, I will.

—

Zoe reminds me of her mother in the way that she laughs and the way that she finds bargains.

But in most ways, she has a lot in common with me.

She's unique and proud, but also a little sad, like The Thridarangar Lighthouse off the coast of Iceland.

—

Zoe and I are parked on a bluff overlooking an RV park.

"What are we doing here?" I ask.

"I just want to see this person your math doodah says is going to go apeshit in a couple of days," says Zoe, pulling a miniature pair of binoculars from her purse.

"Doodah?" I say, a little hurt. "And who's in a Dashiell Hammett novel now?"

"It's totally different. I'm a reporter."

"What happened to fact-checker?"

Zoe is about to roll her eyes when we see him. She watches him through her binocs then hands them to me.

He descends from his dinged-up Streamline like a loping silverback from the Eastern lowlands. Only, instead of a pale night-colored sheen, Geddes sports a blond mullet. He's gripping a can of beer in one hand and a nickel-plated revolver in the other.

"Jesus, he's a walking cliché," says Zoe, taking back the binocs, her face lit up like she just discovered Christmas.

Geddes finishes the beer and places it on a fencepost. He ambles back to the trailer and quickly turns around like a wobbly James Bond before sending a shot wide into the marshland beyond.

Zoe gets out her phone and starts taking video.

I look back into the binoculars.

Geddes takes an unnaturally deep breath, like he is suppressing a mild heart attack. He takes aim and fires once again. This time, the can flips up into the air.

"Well, look at the stable gun enthusiast," says Zoe, not taking her eyes off of him.

—

Driving back to the motel before nightfall, I'm watching a gaggle of Canadian geese rise off the lake as Zoe fiddles with the radio.

"You think it's Geddes, too, don't you?" she asks.

"I don't know. I suppose he's more likely than Manny or Lucinda. Most shooters are white and the youngest was twelve. Nine seems a stretch."

"So, is your math maybe a little bit wrong or what?"

"It's not that simple, Blueberry."

"Dad."

"Sorry. Anyway, predictive models, which the Method is, well, sort of, anyway. It's hard to explain. I mean, I guess what I'm trying to say is that it's as much an art form as it is math. The numbers are constantly shifting. You know, like tectonic plates or your mother's taste in realtors."

"Can we not talk about that right now?"

"Fine with me."

"What else do these numbers tell you?"

"What do you mean?"

"Well, they told you about these names, what else do they tell you?"

"Lots of things."

"Like what?"

"Like there will be thirteen people killed."

"Jesus. And one of these three people is supposed to kill them?"

"I'm not sure. Maybe it's none of them."
"What do you mean, you're not sure?"

"Well, I've never had names just pop up like that. It's one of the things I'm trying to figure out."

"Sure, and the exact location and the exact time and the exact—"

"No, I have the time."

"Really? So, what time is this all going to go down?"

"11:16 a.m."

Zoe looks out the window at a little white boat bobbing on the water.

"Do you think Mom would believe any of this shit?"

I laugh for the first time in days.

32

People tend to have a hard time believing things unless they witness those things firsthand.

Look at the moon landing. Look at the Washington, D.C. UFO incident of 1950.

Hawking, Galileo, Einstein.

A lot of smart people didn't believe them either.

Not that I'm in their league.

My work has the potential to be important one day, obviously, but I'm no Paul Erdős. I could never publish 1,500 mathematical papers in ten Ritalin-filled lifetimes, let alone one. I could never attend the École Polytechnique like a young Poisson did.

I'm just an ex-healthcare marketing executive who was noodling around in his notebook and stumbled upon a way to predict random mass violence. What can I say? I got lucky. Granted, one would have to know a little something about linear, multi-factor regression or probability theory to do what I've done.

So, there's that.

—

I'm not sure what Zoe is thinking, to be honest. Is she humoring me? Is she beginning to believe, but not exactly wanting to?

That was me once.

That was me in the kitchen hearing about the Real Deal for the first time as Marion held a gravy boat.

That was me at that beverage station with the bodies all stacked together like pancakes of human flesh in lifeless green sweaters.

—

Part of me wonders what Marion is up to tonight and part of me doesn't give a rat's ass.

Is she unofficially dating Kevin now? And if they eventually got married, would she take his name?

Marion the Real Deal?

—

But seriously, what the fuck was she thinking? In our shower?

—

Zoe and I are at a pizzeria around the corner from the motel, sharing a medium pepperoni and a couple cans of Budweiser. There's nothing better with American pizza. That's what I've decided. It's the rice-based sweetness of the Bud that perfectly matches all the sugar in American tomato sauce.

Is this my last Budweiser?

Is this my last pizza?

—

"What are you thinking?" I ask Zoe.

"Me? I think I'm just tired. And I have a lot of phone calls to make in the morning."

"About what?"

"About whatever."

"Okay."

"Dad, I'm starting to think either you're not having a midlife crisis, and this is somehow real, or I'm having some sort of nuclear-sized pre-midlife crisis and all of this is complete bullshit."

"Am I supposed to answer that?"

—

I got less and less brave as I got older.

I used to think I could be President.

I used to think I could talk to God.

Who thinks that?

Better yet, who thinks that and doesn't accomplish anything of note?

Mainly, we used to talk about baseball and me not believing in him. Or Him, rather. Doesn't that take confidence? Or delusional balls of grandeur? That's all you need in the end.

Then, you can pay for the horse school in Connecticut.

Then, you can retire before sixty and go to the Seychelles for Halloween.

Then, you can look your daughter in the eye and know she'll never remember you as some kind of sad excuse for a fuck up.

—

When Zoe was a kid, I kissed her goodnight. She would be reading or looking up at the ceiling, and she would be very serious and pucker her lips like I was never going to see her again, which in some way, made me feel that way, too.

—

When I'm gone, she will have sushi without me, and Christmas, and she'll frown the way she does with just one side of her face.

When I'm gone, she will be the only thing on this planet that even remotely cares about anything I ever said or did or looked or smelled like.

—

The Method was all about becoming a better memory for her anyway.

33

"Geddes works at the casino," says a breathless Zoe, holding two lamp-sized coffees in my doorway, bright and early.

"Huh," I say, taking my coffee after having just recently had a dream about dying without an obituary.

"What do you mean, *huh*? Has your method or whatever given you an exact location yet?"

"Not exactly."

"Well, then this might be a contender, no?"

"I suppose," I say, still trying to wake up. "What does Geddes do at the casino?"

"He's a part-time security guard. Plus, divorced with a kid. And he goes to gun ranges religiously. He has an interesting online history. Republican, obviously."

"Hey, you are pretty good at this, Blueberry."

"Dad."

"Sorry. Did you say security guard?"

"Yeah, why?"

"I don't think a security guard has ever been a shooter."

"Well, there's a first time for everything, right? That and he had a real psycho vibe about him. By the way, I got us an appointment."

"An appointment where?"

"At a nearby university."

"To do what?"

"To show this method of yours to a math professor. We have to get on the road right now if we're going to make it."

—

We drive with the windows down.

Big clouds overhead thrust downwards like fluffy fists from heaven. Blind Faith comes on the radio, so I turn it up to think. Do I have anything to say to this professor? Historically, mathematicians have not been kind to each other. It takes years or generations to finally accept a new mathematical process. Not to mention, there are no great mathematicians from Iowa. There are quite a few from Illinois, however, including Robert Andrews Millikan and Ted Kaczynski.

In any case, my daughter has inadvertently given this probably not great mathematician in the middle of Iowa the power to veto everything I've worked on universally.

"So, what exactly did you tell this professor?" I casually scream over the music.

"I told him the magazine I worked for."

"And?"

"And that I wanted him to look at some sort of equation that can predict mass shootings."

"Did you tell him I'm your dad?"

"Nope."

—

How does one's daughter get away with things their wife never would?

They are a reflection of you, for one. The other thing is that youth always gets the benefit of the doubt. Potential is more addictive than cocaine. Parents turn into the King Kong and Flash Gordon of future-casting.

"You'll fucking make it," they whisper-scream into their organic buckwheat pillows from Japan.

—

When I sent that email to the professor at Princeton, I was still looking for acceptance or guidance in some way. I'm past all that now.

Do you teach the winning quarterback how to throw in the fourth quarter?

—

"I talked to Mom last night," she says as we drive past some high brick walls with an idyllic tree-lined drive in front of us.

"Is that right?" I answer as if thoughtlessly conversing with the mailman.

"She was wondering about you."

"Is that right?"

—

Three things no one has ever wondered:

Is regional healthcare marketing more important than Transcendental Number Theory?

Should I quit my job and predict the future in Iowa?

Is Kevin the Real Deal Realtor getting a hand job in my newly renovated shower?

—

Now we're walking through the quad, looking for the mathematics building. Zoe looks excited, the way she used to when I said something particularly smart or funny when her teenage friends were around. The pride would bubble up until she might actually throw an arm around my neck, claiming me publicly, which for a teen is as rare as the giant Tasmanian crab.

"What do you think will happen here?" I ask her.

"Dad, don't worry. In journalism, it's all about multiple sources."

For a moment, I entertain the idea of running for it. Or faking a minor stroke.

"Well, I think this whole idea is silly," I say, taking a deep breath.

—

As we walk down the halls of the university, part of me doesn't feel like I'm completely all there. Not that I'm crazy, but just that I find it hard to concentrate on anything other than what is about to happen.

What will it sound like? What will it smell like? Things like that.

I've noticed it especially with Zoe here. I feel a little withdrawn. I feel a little not me. Or maybe "me" pre-Real Deal. Or maybe "me" pre-not caring whether or not I die a bloody death.

—

TREVOR J. HOUSER

I am an astronaut floating from one motel to the next like far-away space stations. Comforting blurs of light in the great Iowa darkness.

34

The math professor greets us on the stage of an empty lecture hall. Zoe plays reporter while I think about the timing of all this. There are fewer than three days to the Trigger Event. Why am I here? Am I just showing off for Zoe? Am I showing off for myself?

"So, I heard you're working on something interesting," says the professor, who is about my age, but wearing a tight black T-shirt and sporting a tan like he's about to host a TED Talk.

"I think so," I say.

"May I see it?"

I pass him the notebook with the entirety of the Method inside. He casually takes it and opens it like a wine list as he saunters back to his podium.

"Where did you study again?" he asks.

"Woodrow Wilson," I say.

"Where?"

"He didn't study in college," Zoe cuts in. "Which is one of the reasons why I found this story so fascinating."

"So, what got you into math?" asks the professor.

"My wife cheated on me with our neighbor's realtor."

The professor laughs, unsure whether I'm joking or not. "Well, let's see what you have here," he says, turning a page.

"It's all there," I tell him.

"Hm," he says, smiling.

"What?" I ask.

"Oh, nothing."

I look over at Zoe, who is breathless, like this T-shirt professor from Iowa is about to open Capone's safe.

"This is interesting here…I'm not sure how you got this, but I suppose it works…but then, what's this? This can't be right."

"Well, it is right," I tell him.

"There's some interesting thinking here, but I think perhaps you missed a step here." He squints and points to another page in the notebook. "And perhaps there?"

"That's funny," I say.

"Funny how?" says the professor, looking up from the notebook.

I can feel Zoe's eyes drilling holes through me.

"Well," I continue, "I just mean that it's funny you say that because it works."

"Oh really? How, uh, how does it work?"

Zoe steps in. "He only means theoretically that it *should* work."

"No, I mean, it works because I was in Buffalo last month," I say. "I was at the school when it happened. This is what got me there," I say, pointing to the notebook.

"Wait," says Zoe. "The shooting at the community college in Buffalo? You were there?"

The professor puts the notebook down. "I get it. So, basically you just mathematically found out where any random shooting is going to take place."

"Dad, why didn't you tell me this?"

"This man is your father?" asks the professor.

Zoe looks at me, speechless.

"I am her father," I say. Then I pick up my notebook and walk out the door.

—

I'm waiting for Zoe out on the quad when she walks out of the math building. Her cheeks are bright pink the way Marion's get when she's angry.

"What the fuck was that?" she says.

"That was me disagreeing with someone."

"That's not what I'm talking about. This isn't some elaborate father-daughter dinner date anymore. You have to tell the police."

"Tell them what?"

"Why the fuck didn't you tell me about being in Buffalo? Why have you been lying?"

"It's hard to explain, Blue—"

"I swear, Dad, if you call me Blueberry, I'll scream."

This is when I realize two people who were playing Frisbee earlier have stopped playing and are staring at us.

"Do you fucking mind?" I ask the Frisbee gawkers.

The Frisbee gawkers move down the quad near the edge of the math building and safely resume their Frisbee throwing there.

"Listen, this is not how I planned it," I tell Zoe. "It was supposed to just be me."

"And so, what, you were just going to drive around the country until your method got it right? And then what?"

"I would intervene."

"Intervene how?"

"It won't make sense to you."

"Are you just going to stop the shooting by yourself? Is that it? You're going to be some kind of fucking shooting spree hero?"

"What did you think we were doing before this? Did you think it was a joke? I was just out here playing make believe? That's why we came here, isn't it? You thought this professor would show me up and we could wrap this all up and go home to your mom and have a backyard barbecue and be one big happy family around the goddamn Thanksgiving turkey."

"I don't know what I thought."

"You thought your dad was crazy."

"I thought you needed space, but now I think you have some kind of death wish."

"Bingo!"

35

I really do like motel rooms.

Especially brand-new ones. Not new in the sense that they were recently built, but "new" in the sense that I recently pushed my heavy brass key into the lock and opened the door for the first time. There's a universal familiarity there. You find it in all motel rooms, of course, but there are unexpected little details that can be quite gratifying.

Flip-action clock radios.

Gilt-edged bibles.

Styrofoam cups sporting rusty brown coastal sunsets etched on the sides.

For instance, this new motel room I'm currently in has pictures of the English countryside on one wall and two pictures of sperm whales attacking small boats on the other.

Who comes up with this?

Then again, who writes their own obituary?

—

I remember when I was younger on a train. On the way to Chicago. It was cloudy and I was thinking life was romantic or that I could still be Batman and not someone who went into regional healthcare marketing.

I felt like Apollo 11.

I felt like Seattle Slew.

—

Sometimes, I look out the window with half a Singapore Sling and wonder: How did Cary Grant do it? I mean, if you think about it, what are the odds? The lucky bastard.

—

Singapore Sling:

1 ½ ounces gin

1 ounce Benedictine

1 ounce lime juice

¼ ounce simple syrup

2 ounces club soda

½ ounce cherry brandy

garnish with lemon slice

—

I miss the trees bending in the wind. I miss the green drink coasters. My new window looks out on a Home Depot parking lot. There is no pool. There is no retro color scheme. There is no Zoe. No Beth. No Henry.

—

"You don't want to die," you tell yourself your whole life. Or maybe you don't want to live forever, but you want to live long enough. You want to see the Northern Lights. You want to listen to Nina Simone on someone's back deck at two in the morning. You want to stay married to your wife and tell her something nice on your last Christmas together in Palm Desert.

—

"All you see is glory," sang Nina Simone.

—

The thing I remember most from yesterday was that Zoe wouldn't speak to me.

A two-hour drive and she didn't say a word.

When she looked at me, it was with eyes that did not deviate from their death glare locked on the road ahead. Of course, we're so much alike, which will be our downfall. No one forgives. And then we all get old and look ridiculous and it's too late to make up at that point because you're too embarrassed. Why do some people just look out at the world and clench their jaw muscles like we are pioneers of never being satisfied? You know that feeling? When you drive into the Pacific? When you leave your daughter at a random motel in Iowa to fulfill your mathematical death wish?

36

I've done this before. That is to say, needing to clear my head by means of escape. Lots of mathematicians have.

Grothendieck did it in the Pyrenees.

Perelman went to Sweden.

—

Here's something Perelman said:

I'm not interested in money or fame; I don't want to be on display like an animal in a zoo.

I want to believe he yelled that at someone, but I imagine he just wrote it.

Still, good for him.

—

I escaped to Las Vegas when Marion told me she was pregnant.

After finding out they wanted to fire me, I escaped to a nearby park where I could have a panic attack in peace.

—

The last time I escaped was when I was holed up in the study like a madman, writing equations on the walls. Out came the Method. Although I suppose it was even a couple days after that. It was right after Summerville, to be exact. I'd driven all night to see the church with the yellow police tape encircling it and the broken stained-glass windows.

But I couldn't see any bullet holes and all the bodies were gone by then. It was the first time the Method had jumped off the page and showed its face in the physical world. Was it exciting? Yes. But I needed to slow down and think things through. Was the Method for real? Was I really going to do what I thought I was going to do?

—

Marion's family has a big cabin on a lake. That's where I escaped to. It's nice as far as cabins go.

"How do you like Camp David?" her dad, David, would joke every single time we met them there.

Otherwise, her dad was sort of a jerk. He worked for GM and spent most of the time being ruthless on the phone, walking back and forth over the flagstones with a vase of scotch. He gave up on me the moment he realized I wasn't the second coming of Jack Welch.

Marion's mom, on the other hand, was meek and considerate, and I think she possibly even liked me. She was a nationally ranked gin rummy player, which I didn't even know was a thing until then. When she wasn't poring over card strategies, she baked key lime pies and stole pinches of pinot grigio from the fridge while pretending she was washing the dishes.

—

Before Marion and I were married, we would sleep in separate rooms at the cabin.

One time she came in to help me "unpack" so I unzipped my pants and pointed it wildly at her like some fleshy ray-gun set for stun. She laughed. Then she put her mouth on it. But she was only teasing. I mock-grabbed her by the ponytail and said "C'mon," which made her laugh with it still in her mouth. We went down into the woods so that her parents wouldn't hear. I pulled her bikini bottoms around her ankles and I left them there because I liked the way it looked. We did it against an old log like two pioneers in heat. Afterwards, we swam in the lake to cool off. The lake was big, cold, and green. I held her close. The coldness of the lake and the smoothness of her thighs felt good. We watched the smoke from her father's barbecue rise over the treetops like a distant war party. The sun had just set and the sky was all raw gold. I remember a hawk somewhere. Or maybe it was something else. Something hawk-like?

—

Both her parents are dead now and I'll be dead soon, too, I thought, looking at the newly created Method spread across their massive, wagon-wheel coffee table.

—

I didn't know about the soda fountain yet. I didn't know about Oxnard. I was in a cabin near a lake looking at numbers. I was in bed eating cheddar Goldfish straight from the economy-sized carton.

—

One afternoon, I said, "Okay," as if I'd made a handshake deal with the universe.

I was driving past a funeral home when I said this. I'd been noticing it the last few trips into town for supplies and finally pulled into the parking lot.

I didn't even wait in the car or wonder whether it was right or not. I just went inside and looked at a book with photographs of different types of caskets, like Cherrystone Poplar and Economy Silver. Then I looked at a color-coded map of the cemetery.

A young man wearing a gray winter suit that didn't fit quite right said, "You got this red along the highway here and there's blue next to the woods and, well, I guess you could say mint-green down here next to the lake."

I pointed at the mint-green section and someone drove me out there in a shiny black golf cart.

The gravesite I picked out overlooks the lake from a handsome grass slope.

I thought the water looked good from that vantage point. People could look out there and be thoughtful. There were boats and little docks and the weather coming over the Catskills.

The person in the golf cart backed up almost over the ridge so I could relax there and think for a moment. You could tell it was probably protocol, but I thought it was borderline touching.

37

I finally get an email from the Princeton math professor who I sent the Method to all those weeks ago.

Dear Mr. Prumont,

Firstly, I would like to thank you for your fresh thinking in this method of yours. It reminds me that we can't further mathematics without a little risk-taking.

As for the method itself, you come to some interesting conclusions, but I'm afraid the numbers don't add up the way you think they do. You bring up Poisson as one of your inspirations, but I'm not sure I see any correlation between your "method" and anything Poisson discovered.

That said, I'm certain it's been a nice little mathematical diversion for you and I hope you keep trying.

Sincerely,
Dr. Peter J. Sachs

Immediately, I write him back.

Dear Dr. Sachs,

I would pay attention to the news around lunchtime on the 22nd of this month. It might be a nice mathematical diversion for you.

Please talk nice about me when they come to interview you. I even give you permission to say you discovered me.

Warm regards,
Rog Prumont

Blueberry

According to my calculations, I have two days to go.

To mark the occasion, I fix myself Hemingway's Death in the Gulf Stream and sit on my little balcony that, instead of a pool and lovely bending trees, looks out over the Home Depot parking lot and beyond that a sad little creek with a broken-down shopping cart in the middle of it like the *Doña Paz*.

I wonder if Zoe is looking for me or if she's given up on dear old Dad. She is driving home to Marion. To tell her she tried. To tell her, "The old man has completely lost it," while the Real Deal grills steaks in the backyard wearing nothing but my "Best Grillin' Dad" apron.

—

Death in the Gulf Stream:

1 ½ ounces gin

¾ ounce Lillet Blanc

¼ ounce Giffard apricot liqueur

absinthe rinse

—

Part of me is relieved to be free of distraction, but another perhaps even bigger part of me is sad if that was really the last time I'll see her.

"What kind of father does that?" I say to the descending Iowa twilight.

39

My new motel is on the other side of the lake, but you can't see the lake. There is only the idea of the lake. That it exists.

The shooter exists. Only, who knows what side of the lake he's on?

Or if it's really even Geddes?

Or are all those names just another in a long line of mathematical glitches?

Either way, the victims are all at home or on dinner dates or learning about geometry, and either way, all their futures are the same. They are bent and unnatural. People will scream like they did in Buffalo. Or maybe, there was no time to scream.

Maybe the professor was right. Maybe the Method is missing something.

Except it was right once. Almost.

I remember the blood, how sticky it was.

I remember walking down the street like a horror movie extra and just smiling at that kid with her mother and kept walking. "This is how things are in the world," my bloody body told them.

—

I guess he probably knows by now. The shooter, that is. I mean that he probably has an idea of how it's all going to go down. At least, the beginning. He has a face in mind, or perhaps multiple faces. Maybe he's working out something he might even say. Something quotable and properly terrifying. Or maybe it's just a banal manifesto to be found later with his fringe porn collection. That way he can be sure not to leave out anything crucial about the Blacks or the Jews or Rick from marketing.

—

Zoe could've yelled some pretty quotable things at me on the drive home from the professor debacle. When she wants to, she has a mouth like a short-order cook.

Between all the "fucks" and "goddamns," the main point she always seems aimed to get across is that I am being selfish. Obviously, I know this already about myself, but when it comes from Zoe's mouth it hurts nonetheless. For some reason, deep down, I do want to be some Hallmark Lee Majors version of myself for her.

—

What I should've told her is what she wanted to hear. That I would call the police. That she was right to be concerned. Telling her, in effect, that I was looking to go out in a blaze of glory was stupid and put the whole operation at risk. And maybe calling it an operation sounds silly. But still. What if she calls the police? What if she calls Marion?

—

After Zoe yelled at me and I packed up the mobile bar and took a few coasters to-go, I ran into Beth in the parking lot. She was clothed this time, lighting a new cigarette off the old one. I thought there would be an awkwardness between us, but apparently, she had more going on in her life than a bad date with a ballistics soothsayer.

"I'm sorry," she told me.

"About what?'

"About your eye."

"Oh, it's okay," I said, almost forgetting I had a black eye from her ex.

"We're leaving, you know."

"To your sister's?"

"No, farther probably. We've just got to get out of here."

"How's Henry?"

"He was expelled. It's a long story. You know, your basic Christmas card stuff."

I ask her if I can say goodbye to him, but she shakes her head with a knowing sadness, like I was the last one to hear about Pearl Harbor.

"He's at his father's right now."

"Did you agree to that?" I say, suddenly feeling like Perry Mason.

"It's complicated."

"Can you say hi to him for me?"

"Sure. I have to go now."

"I'm sorry."

"I'm sorry, too."

She waved goodbye, and I knew these were our last words.

—

Lewis Carroll's last words were, "Take away these pillows, I won't need them any longer."

"Fuck, a bullet wound," said Sucre.

"I die," said Euler.

—

Eric Harris and Dylan Klebold's last words were "One, two, three!"

Then students hiding in a nearby cupboard heard two gunshots.

—

Zoe's potentially last words to me: "Holy fucking Christ."

40

My new motel is closer to the casino, so I go there for dinner. I get a shrimp cocktail and a ribeye with a bottle of wine. I even bum a cigarette and smoke it out in the parking lot. The day has been a mental Normandy. So many dreams looking vacantly skyward as they bleed out in the surf.

—

I'm explaining to the bartender how to make a Betsy Ross when a policeman walks by, sighing into his CB about someone who would never be the same again because he'd "become a full-blown pussy."

—

I thought of going to the police once.

But I didn't, of course.

It was at a particularly weak point for me during this whole operation. I was like Butch Cassidy in South America. I was like Scottie Pippen in '97.

—

Why do I keep calling it that?

Operation what? Operation Prumont? Operation Go Fuck Myself?

It was probably not long after Buffalo, come to think of it.

When I thought about calling them.

Not long after I walked back to my motel covered in blood.

How many dead people could you stack up on top of each other beneath a soda fountain? For some reason, I feel he probably decided after he shot them. *It would be a good thing to stack them,* he thought. I think it's hard to understand what's going into someone's decision-making during a situation like that.

You make a decision to kill Ferdinand.

You make a decision above Dresden.

—

That girl in the street who saw me, who will grow up and still not make sense of that man walking down the street a bloody mess.

What did her mom say to her?

How does a parent confront the realities of lightweight semi-automatic rifles injected into the vast stresses of job security and some jackass' girlfriend who's decided to move on?

—

I was pretty badly shaken in the days after walking the streets in other people's blood. But then, just as I was getting up the gumption to go down to the station and tell them everything, I realized it was pointless.

What would they say?

They would say, "Thank you, amateur math detective, for letting us know about the next mass shooting."

They would say, "Take this man's notebook and have forensics look into it," and they would throw it in a file somewhere or the trash.

Who believes ex-healthcare marketing people about things like massacres and obscure mathematical theorems?

No one does, except maybe their daughters.

—

Betsy Ross:

1 ½ ounces brandy

1 ½ ounces tawny port

dash of Triple Sec

—

I don't know why I'm drinking so much tonight. More than usual, anyway. I tend to get nervous the day or so leading up to an Event. Sometimes it's drinks. Sometimes it's going to the movies.

Once I got a hooker in Dallas, which was right before Spokane and Buffalo, obviously, except it backfired. Although, really, she was more of a masseuse with an open mind. This was right after I left Marion. I was feeling more vengeful than horny. I cried in the shower before she even showed me her bra.

The open-minded masseuse said, as she packed up to leave: "You're not alone, baby. Everybody's got something going on."

—

What would I have done before the clock tower shooting in '66?

Probably gotten good, authentic barbecue somewhere. Drinks at the Driskill.

On the day of, if my calculations were correct, I'd have waited somewhere on the mall near the old library. That's where most of the shooting took place. Although three were killed nearby on Guadalupe Street, too. I could've waited in the YMCA until the first shots. I could've waited in the bookstore that's no longer there. Or is it?

Even if my calculations weren't spot on, I would've had plenty of time to reach campus and run into the line of fire, trying to shield someone or drag a body to cover.

That's because the whole thing took ninety-six minutes.

It was like the most terrifying horror movie ever in real-time.

—

The first shots fired from the tower weren't until 11:48 a.m., but Whitman had already killed his mother, his wife, a receptionist, and two sightseers inside the tower. Twenty-three minutes before that, he'd arrived downstairs to find that the elevator didn't work.

But an employee gladly activated it for him.

"Thank you, ma'am," said Whitman, wheeling in a footlocker containing seven guns, seven hundred rounds of ammunition, and a machete. "You don't know how happy that makes me."

—

Whitman's last words: "Hi, how are you?"

41

I'm back in my motel, looking in the mirror at a fresh shiner on my other eye.

Also, the doctors have called again.

So has Zoe.

I look at my obituary as I put some ice on my eye and more ice in a tumbler of scotch.

Which I probably don't need at this point.

But then, someone just punched my good eye, so why not?

—

I doubt Poisson ever got a black eye for his distribution theory. Could you imagine Einstein with double black eyes? With that hair?

—

I've only been punched three times in my life. Once in college during a drunken brawl after someone whistled at my date, that punch from Beth's ex, and only minutes ago, when I received a left jab from Spencer Geddes.

—

How it happened was I saw him on guard duty across from the casino bar and, after a couple more drinks, I decided to go over and talk to him. I'm not sure what I was thinking. I suppose more and more over the last couple days the casino has become the number one locale of interest. I was on my way back from scouting all the exits and bumming one more cigarette in the parking lot when I saw him. I suddenly felt the urge to size him up. Before all the panic and hiding in broom closets less than 48-hours away.

I never got to ask those questions of the man in the red windbreaker. Was I making up for it?

"What's up, killer?" I asked him, starting off the conversation in a questionable direction.

"Excuse me?" he asked, trying to remain professional.

I tried to redirect things. I asked him about his gun and if he'd ever had to use it.

"No, thank God," he said.

That's when I asked him, "What if there was a way that you could know days ahead of time whether or not something bad was going to happen in your casino?"

"Bad like what, mister?"

"I don't know, like a robbery or, you know, a shooting."

As the words came out of my mouth, I realized how reckless I was being. It was like Manny all over again, only worse.

What if he'd already made plans? What if I triggered the Event to happen earlier?

Typically, the big shootings aren't last-minute temper tantrums, however. They're obsessed over. It's not always manifesto-level obsession, but it's close. Lurking in the back of their minds, like the Hindenburg.

"I'm not sure what you're selling, buddy, but maybe you should lay off the drinks," said Geddes.

"So, you wouldn't want to know?"

"Know what?"

"Know if someone is trying to tragically alter the course of human history?"

But I could tell he wasn't the intellectually curious type. His eyes glazed over as he resumed his macho security guard stance next to a row of glowing slot machines.

I guess at that point, I accidentally I touched his gun.

Of course, I'm not even sure that I touched it in the sense that I reached out and put my hand on it. But perhaps I got too close when I went to give him a friendly nice-talking-to-you clap on the back. Maybe I came in too low. Part of my arm might have grazed it then. Who knows?

In any case, that's when I wound up on the floor looking up at this potentially homicidal RV nutjob, spitting as he yelled.

—

When they escorted me outside, the sky in the parking lot was a cathedral of stars. I flashed back to fucking Marion in that rain-wet garden behind her best friend's first apartment, loudly whispering "Oh yeah," in her ear, like I was the Shakespeare of garden-fucking.

What will Marion say at my funeral? I wonder.

—

The word "mathematics" only appears in one Shakespearean play, *The Taming of the Shrew.*

Petruchio to Signior Gremio: "I do present you with a man of mine, cunning in music and the mathematics, to instruct her fully in those sciences, whereof I know she is not ignorant."

Not that he really says anything interesting about mathematics, but then some people are afraid of numbers. Even the Bard of Avon.

—

Now I'm having my drink and looking at my numbers. You see, the numbers always change. I have to be vigilant or I could miss something. But really, I'm somehow making up for whatever just happened at the casino. I was never as reckless with the Method as I have been in Iowa.

Is it Zoe being here?

Or did I let my guard down starting with Beth?

Or is it Iowa in general?

I'm so far away from the person I used to be that maybe I'm losing my grip a little. Or because I'm closer to death?

But thinking this annoys me.

This entire phase—even if it's only been so many weeks—has been the most intentional part of my life. But it will also end very abruptly. With an unnaturally bending neck.

Reality is looming.

The Method is close.

—

The Method is a mathematical near-impossibility, but it's also a reminder. Like a letterman's jacket or a scar in the middle of your ball-sack from that time you went spin-casting in a Speedo.

—

I'm not even sure writing my own obituary is a good idea anymore. Why did it seem like such a good idea only a few days ago? I think seeing Zoe in the context of my new situation has loosened my thinking on a lot of things. I remember when I was more rigid as a person. I'd lost my imagination. Life had the mystery of a Hertz rental desk. That's what happens when you swear your life to the pursuit of pretending to be something you are not.

—

Look at Peter Sellers.

Look at Gödel.

—

After my last performance review, Sheila leveled with me: "I don't think you should plan on being here next year, Rog. Friend to friend, there's a lot of changes that will be going on. New blood kind of changes, not to put too fine a point on it. New thinking, if you will."

Sheila, who was not my friend, was drinking from a graphite coffee thermos as big as a capuchin monkey while finishing up an important-seeming text. She never drove a used Saab. She never wrote her own obituary. She was too serious for that. They were all too serious. Everyone walking around the office all day like they were poet laureates or those deep-sea divers that fix things on oil rigs in the middle of Category 5 hurricanes.

"I think this is probably a good time to get things all squared away, if you know what I mean, okay?" said Sheila, her words echoing like a single gunshot in the darkest Iowa night.

42

Once, Zoe asked me if I believed in aliens.

She was eight. There was a campfire and we could hear bats beating overhead like a thousand fly swatters.

I told her I thought there was probably life somewhere in the universe, but that maybe it wouldn't look like it does in the movies.

"I'm afraid of space," she told me, smiling, embarrassed. She had corn on her cheeks and pink and red hearts on her PJs.

"Then you have nothing to worry about," Marion chimed in from the cabin. "Earth is much scarier."

I couldn't see Marion's face because she was unpacking something, but she said this at a time when we had probably already gone past any trajectory where we might safely land whatever blasted off from the middle of that rain-soaked parking lot so many years ago.

Still, in a way, it was the moment I felt closest to her.

Is that sad?

43

If you think you would never do the things you see people in the newspaper do, you're wrong. Especially if you're from Florida. It only takes a little nudge. It only takes a missed paycheck or a misguided weight-scale.

That could be the end of what you knew, right there.

Suddenly, you're having sweet rolls and condensed milk for breakfast as your mother rots in the living room.

—

Does anyone ever think about what the victims ate for breakfast? No, because that's boring. Instead, we mythologize psychopathic shut-ins like they're the Chuck Yeager of mass murder. Because victims aren't fascinating unless they are tragic in some way. They just returned from their honeymoon. They just got a scholarship to play quarterback at Northwestern to fulfill their dying mother's last wish.

Otherwise, victims hold no interest for us because victims are weak and random and because, deep down, we know we could be them.

We know we would be the ones stacked beneath the soda fountain.

We know our last breakfasts could be forever lost like a squadron of torpedo bombers over the Bermuda Triangle.

—

My last breakfast, if anyone cares:

Scrambled eggs with day-old burrata, thick-cut bacon, and mint.

Fujisan bread.

Blood orange screwdriver.

Blue skies.

Phone Call #1

The next morning, I get a call from the doctors.

"Mr. Prumont?" says the doctor. "We've been trying to reach you. We wanted to make sure you were okay."

"Well, I'm not," I say, "but then, you know that."

"Oh, yes, sorry. I'm Dr. Lee with your SCCA team and, really, I suppose we're wondering if you are still intending to go through with the treatment here. At this point, time is not on our side, Mr. Prumont."

"Please, call me Rog. Why don't I come in next week, doc?"

"Yes, the sooner the better," says Dr. Lee. "I'll have our appointment nurse reach out to you later today. How does that sound?"

All of a sudden, I feel as if I'm speaking to Dr. Lee from the frozen rings of Jupiter.

"That sounds fine," I tell her, my voice fading out like a rare and dying radio signal.

Phone Call #2

After breakfast, I get a call from Marion, which for some reason I also pick up.

She wonders when I'm coming home.

Sometimes I wonder. I wonder how much balls it must take for one to be named Kevin and then attach the moniker "Real Deal" to it. I wonder about having a career in real estate and fucking someone else's wife in their recently renovated bathroom. I wonder about whispering, "Oh yeah oh yeah," in her ear. I wonder about being successful.

"We at least need to talk about what we're going to do," says Marion, sounding more like herself than the last call. "I mean, we can't just put everything on pause for the rest of our lives."

"I would say I'm on the opposite of pause right now," I tell her.

"Zoe thinks we're going to make it through this."

"I think you will."

"What does that even mean?"

"It just means goodbye, Marion. I really do wish you the best."

And I hung up realizing that probably was *goodbye*.

And before I start to feel sad about time and space, I get a text from our daughter.

"Im @ Geddes," she says. "4got my cam @ motel. cn u gt?"

46

I wanted to spend my last day sipping on brandy-based cocktails while working the numbers on future death. Gently massaging them. So much changes in the twenty-four hours leading up to the Event. And now, here I am, driving out to Geddes' RV again.

Is Zoe still upset with me?

And why is she still in town?

And why the hell did she go back to the RV park?

—

The camera was easy enough to find, sitting in the middle of her bed. A nice-looking Nikon I got her for Christmas three years ago. Or was that Marion? In any case, as I walked back outside, the strange little pool and the bending trees greeted me like old roommates. It made me realize I'd stayed there longer than most other places, so it felt a little like home.

Monterey was a pretty decent stretch, I suppose, which is how I came to find the farmer's market, which is how I came to be eating that peach when the first shots were fired down in Oxnard.

Spokane, I hardly stayed in at all. I took a taxi ride past Riverside Park and then flew right back to Houston.

Saginaw was a blur.

So was Phoenix.

—

Fourteen people were killed over the course of that peach in Monterey.

A donut peach being the kind of peach that I was eating.

I remember eating it and wondering if it would be my last.

—

I can't recall how long I stayed in Buffalo.

It was probably only a few days, but it feels longer in my mind. The day itself feels interminably long, the way a Catholic wedding feels long, or, I imagine, Antietam.

—

Besides the camera, the other thing I found was a gun. A little Smith & Wesson. It was just sitting there next to the camera.

"Well, look at you," I said to the gun as I slid it into my jacket pocket.

—

As I drive out, the lake flickering in the sun to my right, I wonder if it's me and not the Method. In the sense that the Method is correct, but I'm reading it wrong in some way. Unlike that professor at Princeton, I don't have an assistant. I don't have someone to check my math. I don't have a star pupil named Amber who secretly loves me and will give my eulogy in a tight backless sweater.

Am I missing something? And if so, what?

—

Sometimes I get so caught up thinking about the Method that I forgot about the dying part. Then again, everyone forgets that part.

—

I will miss things like motels.

I will miss cocktail hours.

I will miss seeing my daughter get married and my grandchildren at Christmas and Fourth of July.

I will miss numbers. o

But I won't miss regional healthcare marketing or some twenty-odd years of my life that I walked through like a zombie.

Fuck the Real Deal.

Fuck hard winters.

—

When I get to the bluff overlooking the RV park, I see Zoe's rental car, but no Zoe inside. I begin to feel a prickling sensation coming up from my feet, like static from the carpet. Shooting up through my stomach then fanning out into the distal phalanges like miniature escape pods of panic.

I walk around the car to see if I'm getting something wrong, but there is no Zoe fixing a flat tire. There is no Zoe looking for lost change. I walk around the edges of the bluff and look down, but see no daughters sticking out of the scotch broom or the little ditch surrounding the bluff like a moat. Then I look out over the marshland and see a figure creeping through the RV park in the late-morning mist. I get back into the car and peer through the long lens of the Nikon and see that it's Zoe snooping around the side of Geddes' RV.

I almost honk the horn to get her attention, but then think better of it.

"wht r u doing?" I text her.

"evidence 4 cops."

"wht abt ur camera?"

"2L8. phn wl do."

I look through the camera to see Zoe waving to me across the marshland between us. Then I watch as she opens the door to Geddes' RV and goes inside.

—

Saginaw. Phoenix. Salem. Fort Lauderdale.

Those were sensible places.

Those were places where the Method was free of things like daylight RV raids and headstrong daughters.

—

Paul Erdős once said Japan was very interesting mathematically.

It's difficult to know exactly what he meant by that, but I wouldn't be surprised if he would say the same thing about Little Lake, Iowa.

—

I look at my watch, which tells me Zoe's been inside for almost two minutes now. I look through the long lens and catch a glimpse of her by the window. My daughter. The fact-checking ninja. What is she looking for? A calendar with the date circled in blood? The walls papered over with pages from a first-edition *Mein Kampf*?

Just when I think about driving down to pick her up, I see Geddes pull up in his 1970s-muscle car. He steps out, still wearing the uniform he punched me in. He looks like a character from a Bob Rafelson movie. Someone so doomed they reek of it. As this doomed Bob Rafelson person takes the last few drags from his cigarette, I text Zoe again.

—

"geddes!"

—

I watch Geddes through the lens as he flicks his cigarette and makes a face like he was about to hear the verdict in *The People vs. Fans of Early Chuck Norris*.

He opens the door to his RV and goes inside.

"under the bed," texts Zoe.

—

Through the camera, I watch Geddes as he goes by the window and fetches a beer from his mini-fridge. He untucks his tan guard shirt and looks out the window. I scrutinize his face for any telltale signs of becoming the next Charles Whitman. Distract him, I think. So that Zoe isn't some footnote in Wikipedia.

Do I ram his RV? Yell "fire"?

As various scenarios flip through my mind, Geddes leaves the window and a moment later, I get another text.

"!!!"

I look back through the lens to see a bare-chested Geddes coming back towards the window, holding Zoe by the wrist. He sits her down on something,

Is he is interrogating her?

He takes the phone out of her hand. He looks down at it, scratches his head, and then turns around suddenly. He looks out the window. Looking in my direction now. My phone buzzes.

On the screen, it says "Blueberry."

"Hello?" I answer.

"Who is this?" says Geddes, sounding drunk.

I tell him it's all a mistake.

"You're goddamn right it is."

Then he hangs up.

—

"Your father was a great man," is something I imagine Zoe hearing years later as I hurl myself down the side of the bluff and fall face first in swamp water.

After sloshing around like a drunk Bear Grylls, I finally make it to the RV and pound on the door.

I tell myself I will not die just yet, and that my obituary is not at that very moment transforming into some sad and obscure absurdity destined for the margins of the *New York Post*.

I go to the door of the RV and knock on it. Geddes answers.

I have the gun from Zoe's bed still in my jacket pocket.

"I have a gun," I tell Geddes, not taking it out.

"So do I," says Geddes, unimpressed.

"Where is she?"

"You two are together? Are you with my ex or something? Did she fucking put you up to this?"

"She's my daughter."

"Get in here," he tells me.

I go inside. Zoe is sitting on a couch looking at me like she's just realized she's on the wrong flight but is too embarrassed to get off.

"Jesus Christ," says Geddes, finally recognizing me. "It's you. From the casino. I just got fired because of you, goddamnit."

"Sorry," I say. "I think my daughter and I should probably just go."

"I told him I went in the wrong trailer, but he wouldn't listen," says Zoe hopefully.

"You know what I think?" says Geddes. "I think you two are trying to frame me. Trying to frame me so I lose custody of Spencer Jr."

"Who?" asks Zoe.

"My son."

"Your son's name is Spencer?"

"Now you're fucking with me," says Geddes.

—

The first thing I thought when Zoe was born was that I can't be a failure. I just can't. Everyone is doing better. They're becoming VPs and taking trips to the Maldives. Building memories and confidence.

At one point, I remember threatening Marion that I'd go to work as a bartender in Qatar if I couldn't make enough money in the U.S.

That's the epiphany you have with kids.

That none of it will ever be enough, and sooner or later, they'll be old enough to see you for who you really are. No one wants their children to look at them through the unflinching prism of adulthood. How you had to move out of the big house and rent the little apartment next to the park with the used condoms and crushed beer cans. It becomes sad in a subtle way that's hard to explain, but you can sense the sadness. You didn't take her friends out to the moderately priced steak house. You took three of her friends to a ballgame one year, and then just one friend the next. It's small, but also it isn't. Before, I was always thinking the worst-case scenario won't happen. But it will. It always does. Look at the Bhutan Death March. Look at Deepwater Horizon.

—

Just when I'm not exactly sure where this conversation with a drunk Geddes can go from here, someone knocks on the door.

"Who is it?" says Geddes

"Mr. Geddes? It's Officer Rollins."

For a split-second, Geddes looks around the RV in a panic, but decides to open the door with his shirt off and two quasi-hostages anyway.

"What is it, officer?" he says.

"Jenny called down to the station and said you came over to see the boy unannounced this weekend," answered Rollins. "And you know we can't be doing that Mr. Geddes, am I right?"

Just then, Zoe takes my hand and butts in between the cop and Geddes at the door.

"Well, sounds like we should be going, Dad," she says matter-of-factly. "Thanks for letting us look at the car, Mr. Geddes."

The policeman looks quizzically at the two of us emerging from the RV, and then back at Geddes, who is speechless.

"You getting rid of Mongo?" the cop asks him.

"No," says Zoe jauntily before Geddes can speak, "but we thought we'd haggle over it just the same. Have a good day, officer."

"Hold up," says the cop. "What happened to you?" He's looking at me.

"Oh," I say, realizing I'm dripping wet. "I fell. In some water."

"No, mister, what happened to your eyes?"

Suddenly, I remember my double black eyes.

"These? These are old, officer," I say, pointing to them. "This one is from someone's ex and this one is from someone else's ex," which I realize is basically true.

"Well, don't we live in exciting times?" says Officer Rollins. "You better keep your daddy out of harm's way there, miss."

"Don't I know it?" says Zoe, laughing nervously as we quickly walk away.

—

Back at the car, she asks me if I really had a gun.

"You mean yours?" I say, pulling it out.

"Jesus, I need a drink."

"What time is it?"

"Very fucking funny."

47

Up until I was eleven or twelve, I still thought becoming Batman was a viable career option. Not with the cape and the ears and all that jazz, but a ninja-like vigilante with a bulletproof car seemed reasonable to me.

All I needed was to get rich and do the training.

Is that pathetic?

The answer is yes, of course, but it's other things too.

—

Einstein wanted to be a fireman.

Gödel wanted to play third base for the Cincinnati Red Stockings.

Who can say otherwise?

—

One of the kids in Buffalo apparently wanted to be a fireman. I saw it in the newspaper a couple days after. He majored in drama, but his dad was a firefighter. He liked to go camping and had a younger sister named Rebecca. His body was second to the bottom, if I remember correctly. Blue plaid smooshed between a loose gray sweatshirt and something denim-like.

—

Freudenthal probably saw some things in that concentration camp in Havelte. He was a Dutch mathematician.

Trachtenberg definitely saw things.

—

Like a writer, I imagine things a mathematician might see influences their math in some way. Why wouldn't it? Numbers can absorb human suffering. Unlike words, numbers are emotionless and therefore can handle untold amounts of human tragedy, like Hiroshima or the *USS Indianapolis.*

—

Unlike Saginaw, Phoenix, Salem, Fort Lauderdale, and Spokane, Little Lake, Iowa is a place that will be remembered forever because of numbers.

Zoe will point it out on a globe to my future grandchildren and tell them that's where it all happened.

"That was your grandfather," they'll hear her say for the three-hundred and forty-seventh time.

—

I don't know what Marion would think about all this.

Or Poisson or Gauss or Erdős, for that matter.

About the places I've been or what I'm doing. Would they have walked down the street covered in blood? Would they have stood in the middle of that farmer's market, eating a donut peach, waiting to be shot?

But then, most mathematicians aren't action heroes.

Not that I'm either of those. Not professionally, anyway.

But I am out here.

I am working on a "math thingy" that could change the world.

I am walking into Midwestern RVs with concealed weapons.

48

My wife is the Goldbach Conjecture.
    My daughter is the Diophantine Equation.
    I am Batman.

49

Zoe orders a margarita and I order a Blue Hawaiian. You only live once.

"When did you get the gun?" I ask her.

"I think last year."

"But why?"

"Oh, Dad," she says, taking a sip, looking so much like my daughter. "Have you read a newspaper lately?"

—

Blue Hawaiian:

1 ounce light rum
1 ounce blue curacao
1 ounce cream of coconut
2 ounces pineapple juice
pineapple wedge
maraschino cherry

—

Zoe had a weird thing with alcohol when she was younger, in that she was overly repulsed by it.

"I can smell the chardonnay," she would declare to Marion before removing herself from the room.

In movies, if the characters were imbibing, she would recoil in horror.

When the *Three Amigos* had glugs of tequila in that bar where half the locals got shot up by Germans in Easter clothes, she ran from the room as if it were *The Texas Chainsaw Massacre*.

Not because of the violence, but because of the booze.

—

"Why didn't you tell the police?" I ask her.

"The situation wasn't right," she says.

"Are you still mad at me?"

"An anonymous tip would be better."

"So, you are still mad at me."

"Besides, something about the Spencer Jr. thing bothered me."

"You're mad at me."

"Yes, I'm fucking mad at you. And I just almost got killed by a future mass murderer."

"You're right."

"I'm right about what?"

"I'll call the police."

"Dad."

"What?"

"Why do you want to?"

"Why do I want to what?"

"Kill yourself?"

The waitress suddenly appears with a giant plate of nachos. Her expression is like that of a meter-maid accidentally walking into the situation room during the Cuban Missile Crisis.

"This is what we call the Naughty Boy, for some reason," says the waitress, looking meekly at the chips covered in cheese and black beans.

"They were going to fire me, you know," I say after the waitress hurries away.

"What?" asks Zoe.

"They told me before I left town that I was done. That was months ago."

"But that happens to people all the time."

"Yeah, except I hated my job for twenty-odd years, and now I'm almost sixty. You don't start over at my age. Plus, your mother and I haven't had sex since Christmas of 2018. I don't have enough money to retire on. There's no summer in Zürich. There's no money for you or any future little Zoes. If Marion runs off with the Real Deal, you'll have to sell the house and you'll get shit for it because we never kept it up. I've done nothing with my life, Blueberry."

"Jesus, Dad."

"Plus…"

"Plus what?"

50

Galois died of wounds from a duel.

Gödel died of starvation, convinced people were out to poison him.

—

What will Prumont die of?

An AR-15?

Malignant tumors in the large intestine?

Becoming the Genghis Khan of health marketing comebacks?

—

Zoe looks shaken.

"Dad, why didn't you ever say anything?"

"About what?"

"About all of it?"

—

Failure is never really discussed. Not in this epoch, anyway.

I can't recall the last time I talked about failure with Zoe, or really, anyone for that matter. Is it more difficult to talk about failure when you're in the middle of failing?

—

Columbia University has an entire school dedicated to failure.

Except they call it the Education for Persistence and Innovation Center, which of course sounds much better than the Graduate School of Collapse and Inadequacy.

One study found that high school students performed better on tests after hearing of the intellectual struggles of Einstein and Marie Curie.

"It's fine to celebrate success, but it is more important to heed the lessons of failure," the 15th richest person in the history of the world once said.

—

I say to Zoe, "It's okay."

She's possibly trying to cry into my shoulder. We are somehow on a bench now.

"How long have you known?" she asks.

"Sometime before my birthday."

"So, like, it's terminal?"

"Yeah."

"Does Mom know?"

"No."

"How come you didn't tell me till now?"

"I think I was just sort of locked into the ending of whatever this is," I say, not really sure what any of that means.

—

I think about driving off towards Summerville all those nights ago. I was no longer a husband or a father or anything recognizable at that point. I was a kinetic projectile. My heart was made of lead.

—

I would give Zoe everything if I had it, but for me, the chance for success turned out to be less than the survival rate of frogs in space.

There will be no second home on the Cape.

There will be no private family doctor.

Just because your bar is set dangerously high doesn't make it any less heartbreaking.

—

We are walking somewhere by the lake, the sun dipping into it like a dying volcano.

"Want to go for a swim?" I ask her.

"I don't think I'm ready for bad jokes yet, Dad."

—

On the drive back to my new motel to get my stuff, Zoe looks out the window with the expression of someone who just saw the second plane hit.

"What made you change your mind?" she asks.

"About what?"

"Calling the police."

"Well, Blueberry, if you think what I'm doing is reckless or selfish, then what's the fucking point?"

"You really thought it would work?"

"What? Arrive precisely at the time and place of a mass shooting and die while trying to save lives?"

She smiles at me, her eyes red, "Okay, sorta funny."

—

I am selfish, after all.

But so was Scottie Pippen. So was Björk.

Who isn't when they're dying? Pets run off to the woods all the time to die by themselves. Maybe they're onto something. Maybe I'll just walk off into the woods. I'll bring a bottle of Armagnac and something good to read.

—

I ask Zoe, "What threw you back there about the name?"

"The what?" asks Zoe.

"What was it about Geddes having a son with the same name?"

"Oh, well, I mean, does your method account for things like namesakes?"

"What do you mean?"

"How do you know the Spencer Geddes your method conjured up wasn't supposed to be Spencer Geddes Jr.?

I take a breath like I'm about to destroy a good tennis racket.

"What time does it happen again?" asks Zoe.

"11:16 a.m."

"I'll think about it."

"Yeah, I need to do some work, too."

—

The name thing bothers me because I was always expecting just one. Is it a glitch? Is it fucked?

I always anticipated exact coordinates and a time. How do numbers know the difference between a father and a son?

—

We drive under Iowa stars along a road where future funeral processions will snake by in glittering black cars. I see a church, but it doesn't make me think of God. The closest I ever came to God was in Buffalo. That exact moment in time seemed holy in a way. It was like He had just been there. The green sweater with that curl of blonde hair. It was a sacred thing not meant for the eyes of the living.

—

I will call the police, but tonight is the last night. I didn't come this far to go out with a whimper. Besides, I'm not going to die in some hospital or back home with Marion fussing around, feeling guilty. Horrifically is the best way to go. Patton probably said that. Or someone like Patton. You could see him saying it matter-of-factly to his troops or to the President. In any case, it feels better knowing someone like that might've agreed with the sentiment. In any case, it will be over. Either way.

—

Back at the motel, I do the numbers and Zoe makes some calls.

Then it's late.

"Will you sleep next to me, Dad?" she asks.

"Of course, Blueberry."

It's like when she was a little girl. Marion and I would take turns sleeping with her when she had nightmares. She was frightened all the time. Of spiders. Of dogs. Of the nightly news.

"I'm sorry I ruined your plans," she says through a yawn.

"I'm glad you did," I say, looking out at the bending trees and the moon.

—

I like motel rooms at night. Little microwaves and alarm clocks glow like Andromeda. My daughter and I, comfy and contained, like a young Shepard and Schirra.

—

Part of me wonders if any of this makes sense. Perhaps I should've never left Marion. Perhaps I should've just made peace with it. Invited the Real Deal over to a neighborhood block party and buried the hatchet.

Whose relationship ends this way?

Cheating in the shower on the eve of your husband's birthday? Keeping your terminal cancer a secret? Becoming a math hermit?

—

"What happened over there?" asked a college student, who was crying and pointing towards a vague area of campus I had just walked from.

"I don't know," I said, covered in blood.

"Do they need help?"

"No."

—

In the middle of the night, I put my arm around Zoe while she is sleeping. I kiss her hair the way I used to when she still wore her lacrosse uniform to bed.

How do they get so grown up?

The mother of the girl in the green sweater probably thought the same thing at one point. She was a living thing with a possibly bright future. Before her daughter's neck bent unnaturally. Before the soda fountain.

"Goodnight, Blueberry," I whisper into the vast motel darkness.

51

The police aren't sure what to make of me the next morning.

"Sir, you are aware there is no red flag law in the state of Iowa?" says the officer over my last burner phone.

"What does that mean?"

"Well, it means we don't just pick people up because some anonymous person calls up worried some guy's gonna go shoot someone."

"Well, all I know is he intends to shoot up the goddamn casino this morning, so if you'd rather speak to him over a pile of dead bodies, that's up to you fellas."

I hang up feeling rather good about swearing to the police so casually, like I was Dirty Harry.

—

I met him once, Clint Eastwood. I was in a bowling alley in Sun Valley when I was ten. I was with a friend of mine who had a cast on.

He came up in his dark-blue ski jacket and asked her, "What happened to your arm there, little lady?"

It was Clint Eastwood and he actually talked like that. Or he was just playing to type for the kids. He possibly had a beer in hand, but I can't be sure.

I can't remember what she said either.

Probably, she just laughed nervously and tells the same story I do.

—

I realize the person I was most of my life is already dead. I am looking at the motel rug when I think this. When you become a different version of yourself, other people tend to call them chapters, but that's really just trying to make it seem like it's easier than it actually is.

—

Who in Little Lake, Iowa knows where to find burrata and Fujisan bread at this hour? But I do have blood orange juice and vodka, so I make a nice screwdriver.

Zoe is somewhere on her phone.

I've taken a chair outside the room so I can look down at the pool in the sunshine with the trees and the shed marked ONLY! A good cocktail and sunshine are things that make me concentrate, which is what I need, because I'm pretty sure the Method is trying to tell me something.

But what?

—

Not that it's abnormal for someone to struggle in their work.

Smale had his troubles in undergrad before receiving the Fields Medal in '66.

Galois twice failed to get into the École Polytechnique.

—

I'm finishing my drink when I realize the Method has produced another name.

Annie Reid, I write down in my notebook.

And then another.

Gregory Davies.

And then another.

And another…

—

I remember eating that peach in Monterey, thinking I was going to die. It was just going to happen and I was ready for it. It would be like light hitting water, or the 2:26 mark on the Cowboy Junkies cover of "Sweet Jane." And then came Houston and Spokane and the rest, and I began to question things.

There was no light hitting water. There was no Cowboy Junkies.

In a way, I feel less ready now.

Things were happening so fast in the beginning.

—

Not Churchill, not Roosevelt, but a spitfire pilot said, "The worst part was the waiting."

52

I have Zoe's gun in my pocket.

It feels like a small but heavy camera that can put holes the size of dimes in people.

But the idea of shooting myself doesn't feel the same for some reason.

Less heroic? More depressing?

I'd been thinking about it happening in one way for so long now it's hard to switch gears. But I think I also forgot, with everything going on, how much I enjoyed Zoe's company. Not that the doctors can do anything.

But maybe we could extend the road trip awhile longer. Eke out a few new memories. Just the two of us.

We could go anywhere.

53

"I think maybe we fucked up," says Zoe.

She says this as she walks hurriedly down the outside corridor towards me and my Alabama Slammer.

"What do you mean?" I ask, sensing the need to sit up straight.

"What if it's not the casino?"

"I don't have the exact location, but it has to be Geddes."

"Why does it have to be?"

"It just makes sense. Listen, the Method can only give us so much information."

"I understand that, Dad, but Geddes' kid has the exact same name."

"So?"

"So how do we know it's not the kid? Not to mention, Lucinda is a kid."

"I'm not following."

"There are two kids on your list of names who are under twelve and no one younger than twelve has ever been a shooter, right?"

"Yeah, that's right. Except the list just got longer."

"What do you mean longer?"

"Blueberry, things always change last minute."

"How many names?"

"There's nineteen now."

"So, it's gotta be wrong, right?"

"Well, maybe it's Manny," I say hopefully. "He's a gun owner."

"Manny has a kid, too. And that kid and Lucinda and Geddes Jr. all go to the same school."

She dials something on her phone.

"Give me one of the new names on your list. Just any name. Give me two."

I look at the names in my notebook.

"Okay, Brooke Hillyer and Reece Davis."

"Yes, hello, is this Little Lake Middle School?" Zoe asks in her best perky-mom voice. "Great, hi, this is Mrs. Hillyer, you know, Brooke's mom. Can you remind me what time her lunch hour is today? I forgot it and need to drive over…I see…yes, at eleven-oh-five. And is that the same time for Reece? Sorry, Reece Davis? I have his lunch, too…yes…okay, thanks. I'll be over soon!"

She hangs up and looks at me like we just won whatever the reverse of the lottery is.

"They're not possible shooter names," I say before she can. "They're victims."

"Holy shit," says Zoe.

I finish the rest of my drink and check the numbers again.

That's when the Method gives me one more name.

"What is it?" asks Zoe.

"Oh, nothing," I say.

54

"Roger Prumont," says the Method.

55

I should feel excited.

If this were a week ago, I would've been thrilled. I would've made a final Wallbanger and strode out into the sunshine feeling like professor Hao Huang after resolving the Sensitivity Conjecture.

But now I'm conflicted.

I want to hang around for a few more weeks.

Spend time with my daughter.

Not get shot in the face.

—

"Be sure you're not making it about you," Marion would probably say.

—

After realizing he slept an extra fifteen minutes each night, de Moivre calculated the exact time of his death. The point at which he would have amassed twenty-four hours of "extra" sleep. That happened on November 27th, 1754.

—

"The smell of death surrounds you," said Ronnie Van Zant.

—

I think Zoe would want to see something like the Herbert Hoover Presidential Library. It's not far at all.

I mean, wouldn't she? With her dad. Why wouldn't she?

She could ask about details of my life. I could tell her about the Jeep stuck in the Pacific while leaving out the part about the girl in the cutoffs. I could tell her about the farmer's market in Monterey and the deathless peach.

When I tell her, we would be driving in pink twilight, so pink it's almost green, like the skin of a gator tumbling through the troposphere and the noctilucent clouds.

We would be driving towards the American Gothic House in Eldon.

Or the Maquoketa Caves in Jackson.

We would be laughing and temporarily hopeful.

56

In Buffalo, I hugged the bodies.

It's hard to explain.

First, what I did was see if anyone was breathing and then, for some reason, I found myself sort of hugging the pile of bodies.

It wasn't a decision I made. It was more like a visceral reaction, really. I can't say what I was thinking exactly. I do remember an overwhelming feeling of being in a sacred place.

Like Machu Pichu or Ground Zero.

I'm not much of a church-goer or even that interested in religion, but I do feel a sort of reverence when I step inside a chapel for a wedding or a funeral. That's what it felt like at that moment. Just me alone with these people who were no longer people exactly. I don't know. I was crying and hugging them. Then I sat down and looked at the girl's green sweater with that curl of blonde hair over the collar. The one that could've been Zoe's age. I never wanted to see her face. I'm not sure who I'd be right now if I'd seen her face. In any case, as I sat there, I must have been sitting in quite a lot of blood. Or kneeling in it. That, along with the hugging, must've been what soaked me. Then I heard the sirens and I walked out into the streets like the patron saint of firearm-related violence.

I will never come here again, I thought.

—

In one first grade classroom at Sandy Hook, every student was killed except one.

When police finally got to her, the six-year-old told them, "I'm scared and I want to go home."

57

I find myself making a Harvey Wallbanger as Zoe reads aloud the names of the future mass shooting victims of the United States of America.

"Now what the fuck do we do?" she asks, looking completely lost for the first time in her life.

"Sit down," I tell her.

Then I hand her the drink and walk out the door.

—

What would the girl in the jean cutoffs think? What happened to that boy she met in Mexico? Where is he going? Why does he have a gun in his pocket?

—

I walk past the ice machine. Down the steps into the sun-blasted parking lot. From the pool, I can hear someone playing the Cure. Who plays the Cure anymore? Who plays the Cure in a two-star motel in Bumfuck, Iowa?

Then I remember Huey Lewis and the News was playing during the last Trigger Event. That was only over a week ago. It happened just outside Pittsburgh, in West Mifflin, except I was just a little more outside Pittsburgh in a town called Seven Springs.

It was in a parking lot, too. Some old man playing checkers by himself. Except it was the parking lot of a predominantly Black church. I did get that right. Only, it was a predominantly Black church in West Mifflin, obviously.

—

It was an out-of-work fishing guide that went apeshit.

Apparently, he had swastikas painted down in his basement or possibly his grandmother made out with Himmler.

Something fucked up, anyway.

"Might as well blame neo-Nazism on guns too," joked the bartender while looking up at the TV later that evening.

At least, I think it was a joke.

This was in Seven Springs and I'd had a few drinks already, wondering why I wasn't dead in West Mifflin.

I wouldn't know about Little Lake, Iowa for at least another 36 hours.

I was drinking a Georgia Mule in the Foggy Goggle Method gave me that one.

—

Georgia Mule:

1 peach slice, skinned

1 ½ ounces vodka

½ ounce fresh lemon juice

2 dashes peach bitters

ginger beer

—

Five people died in West Mifflin.

One of them was a new dad who was shot in the face.

One of them was a dog-lover who bled-out through her groin area.

—

Other places people have been randomly shot in the face:

A garlic festival

Baseball practice

Chuck E. Cheese's

Middle school dance

Buddhist temple

Bowling alley

Welding shop

Football watch party

Jewelry store

Block party

Hospital

Line dancing

Madden NFL 19 competition

Art festival

Waffle House

Public library

High school house party

Planned Parenthood

Live TV interview

Sorority house

International airport

Spa

Power plant

Amish schoolhouse

Haunted house

Howard Johnson's

Lockheed Martin

Xerox

Tulsa

—

Beth answers the door with red, sleepless eyes.

"Why are you still here?" I ask her.

"Jesus, who gave you the second shiner?"

"Oh, this?" I say touching my black eye. "It's nothing. But I thought you were leaving town."

"I thought so, too. It's a fucking logistical nightmare. On top of that, Henry ran away to his dad's house last night. Guess the bottom dropped out on mom stocks. We should've left last week."

"Wait, is he at school?

"Honestly, I have no fucking idea, Rog, and I'm not really in the mood."

"You have to get him out of the school, Beth."

"Why?"

"Something bad is going to happen."

"What are you talking about? What does 'bad' mean?"

"Just get him, okay? I'm going there now."

—

Am I going? Why am I going? I was going with Zoe to the American Gothic House in Eldon. Then to the Maquoketa Caves in Jackson. That was the plan in my head, anyway. We were going to eat a nice steak dinner at a chop house somewhere, then walk around and look at all the goddamn gothic revival architecture. Or is everything fucked now? And if everything is fucked, how fucked is it?

—

I'm vibrating with possibilities. I'm being pneumatically discharged to achieve sufficient launch velocity.

—

"I saw you look like a Japanese baby," Robert Smith croons across the parking lot. "In an instant, I remembered everything."

—

Back in the room, I find Zoe sitting on the edge of the bed, her drink nearly finished.

"Did you call the police?" I ask her.

She shakes her head no. Without a word, I take her by the wrist and lead her down to my car.

The dash clock reads 10:58 a.m.

"Call 911," I tell her.

"And tell them what, exactly?"

58

In mathematics, beauty and elegance are intrinsic. Which is to say, in the purest sense, numbers are beautiful in the way nature is beautiful. So, one must see the fast Fourier transform or Euclid's theorem in the same way one sees stars or a Kodiak bear crashing through the fog.

Then again, math can be an earthquake or a wolf spider just the same.

The Method scared me at first. Like a beautiful girl who speaks Danish.

But only briefly do you feel this way.

You know the feeling you got the first time you saw the shark in *Jaws*? It was terrifying, but it also thrilled you. Things can be beautiful and terrifying at the same time.

Look at quantum mechanics.

Look at Marion.

—

I remember staring at it on my coffee table when I was finished.

The Method, that is.

Even before I understood its mathematical implications, I knew it was my ticket out of there. No more Real Deal. No more getting into my car and wanting to drive into a burning gas station.

The scarier thing to think about is what I would have done without it.

Move onto a friend's couch?

Take Marion back and happily shower every night where the Real Deal gripped her from behind like a bouncing machine gun of freckled flesh?

—

"I know numbers are beautiful," said Erdős. "If they aren't beautiful, nothing is."

—

But would Erdős speed through a red light with his already-traumatized daughter? Or, for that matter, would Gauss or Poisson run towards the future site of a national tragedy like mathematical first responders?

—

Poor Zoe.

She's looking flustered and no doubt processing so many things as we speed past the lake.

I taught her how to ride a bike next to a lake like this one, actually.

Smaller perhaps, but the same general idea. Oval-like with some boulders and a smattering of trees at one edge, looking almost too perfect, like something from a train set. We were somewhere near the coast. The smell of Cascara buckthorn and cigars. That's because it's the one place Marion would let me smoke them. Something about the sea air. Or maybe it was that she drank more. I remember having to throw the maduro down in the grass lining the pathway whenever Zoe lost control. Dad to the rescue. Steadying her back seat with one hand, the other on her handlebars. It went like this for what seemed like an hour when suddenly she just zoomed along and laughed and never looked back as she faded into the darker part of the evening.

—

Zoe has called the police and is now looking out the window at the lake. She looks like someone just tried to explain quantum field theory to her.

"How can I freeze like that?" she says to the windshield.

"What do you mean?"

"Dad. Back at the motel. If I'm going to make it as a goddamn journalist, I can't just freeze like that. What journalist freezes at the apex of a story like that?"

"Maybe one whose father is the story?"

"Did you really think I would be disappointed in you?" she asks.

"About what?"

"About losing your job or not having enough money or whatever."

"Well, maybe 'disappointed' is the wrong word. It's more your idea of me. You'd be surprised how much you change your opinion about someone without even consciously deciding to."

"Dad—"

"I just mean as you get older, you realize the importance of things you accomplish or attain depends almost entirely upon how people you care about perceive those things."

"Jesus, Dad. But you wanted to kill yourself."

"I know, but that's what I'm saying. Pretty fucked up, right?"

—

Sometimes I wonder: if there wasn't any cancer and I somehow saved my job and the Real Deal never existed, would I be doing this? Would I have this secret life? This life of driving from town to town, trying to solve deadly mathematical mysteries? It takes a certain amount of unhinging to dive headlong into something that crazy. Extramarital affairs. Being a hitman. Undertakings like those call for attention to detail and the ability to compartmentalize. To slip from one life to the other without bringing anything with you or leaving anything behind.

Would I have taken fake business trips or only pursue leads on the weekends?

Would I still have wanted to die?

And, more importantly, would I have been raising false alarms from the California coast to Seven Springs?

Although I suppose it's all a moot point because I never would have hatched the Method in the first place. All those dumb and terrible things had to happen the way they did. Doom begets doom.

—

"So, tell me about this boyfriend of yours," I say to Zoe as the trees blur by faster and faster now.

"Why do you care about that right now?"

"Just curious. Is this guy the one or what?"

"Dad, this is why I don't talk to you about this stuff."

"Do you ask your mom for relationship advice?"

This makes her smile.

"Well, when you put it that way."

"So, is it serious?"

"I don't know if it's serious for him."

"But is it serious for you?"

"Yeah, I guess."

"What's his name?"

"Land."

"Land?"

"Dad."

"Do you love the guy?"

"Shit, I guess."

"That's good."

"Look how it worked for you."

"Falling in love is nice."

"I guess."

—

I pull up to the school. No sirens yet. No screaming.

"Where are you going?" Zoe asks when I get out.

I make up something about meeting the police inside, which I don't think she buys, but she's too bewildered and concerned to press me.

"Where will I meet you?" she asks as I lean down to her open window.

"Back at the motel."

"Our motel?"

"Yep. By the way, do you think you could take more time off work?"

"You mean right now? Wait, why?"

"I thought maybe we could visit a few towns on the way home. Have a couple nice dinners. Make a trip of it."

"Dad, is everything going to be okay?"

"You bet," I tell her.

And then I kiss her on the forehead like I used to when she woke up from a nightmare.

59

The biggest mass shooting in the United States was Las Vegas in 2018.

58 killed and 851 injured.

There were only 32 Americans killed in the Battle of Bloody Gulch.

Just 2 in the Battle of An Lão.

—

Of all the mathematicians running around Europe during World War II, it's hard to believe only three were killed by the Gestapo. Of course, a fourth killed himself after being summoned by them.

Imagine that letterhead being the first thing you see on a Saturday.

Paul Epstein was his name.

He knew a thing or two about number theory. Not sure if he had a daughter. Or any kids, for that matter. Maybe he had no one and everyone hated him. Maybe he was beloved by the entire village of Dornbusch.

Other mathematicians were probably killed by the Gestapo, except they weren't historically significant. That's the thing. Are you historically significant enough? Are you meaningful in a way that it would be wholly unacceptable to *not* be counted in a death toll for your chosen profession?

Would regional healthcare marketing remember you?

This is what I was trying to explain to Zoe.

Everyone has a gravesite, but not all of them are marked.

This feels vaguely profound, like something Sitting Bull or perhaps Sting might say. Or maybe it's not that profound. Maybe it's only something William McKinley might say after his third McKinley's Delight.

—

McKinley's Delight:

3 ounces rye whisky

1 ounce sweet vermouth

2 dashes cherry brandy

1 dash absinthe

—

Honestly, I'm probably not even a Paul Epstein.

Am I a Stanisław Saks?

Am I a Juliusz Schauder?

60

I go through the main doors to the front office, but no one is there.

As I walk down the hallway, I hear the sirens in the distance like the expanding whine of approaching Stuka dive bombers.

"I am Dunkirk," I say to myself.

I look at a map on the wall and find a bright red square marked "Cafeteria." I start walking towards the bright red square. There are banners on the walls and pictures of smiling yellow suns and fire-breathing dragons.

You can hear the children screaming now.

One of them squirts out the double doors and runs past me down the hallway, the color drained out of her face.

There's a loud bang, but it's not the doors slamming behind her. It sounds like Buffalo. It sounds like Guadalupe Street.

It feels as if I am walking through gelatin. Like a dream, the air feels heavier. The air feels like translucent osmium.

It seems odd, suddenly, that I am here. Walking through translucent osmium in a school in Iowa towards all that noise. I should be taking up soul-cycling or mentoring at-risk children. Instead, I've got a gun in my pocket and I'm walking towards this place of extreme loudness.

Who is this man with the gun and the no-nonsense stride?

He must lead a daring life and know multiple languages.

I imagine this is what the teachers think as they peer through their little windows in the classroom doors, clutching their paper weights and staplers.

I should've been a teacher. I should've taught math. I have a friend from college who teaches English all over the world. Bolivia, Hungary, you name it. He simply moves to whichever exotic town he feels like and teaches there for a few months, maybe sleeps with a woman or two, then moves on to the next town, the next continent.

There he is, hiking in a lush mountain valley.

There he is dancing, with two girls under a roof of palm fronds.

Here I am, opening the double doors.

Look at me, Erdős!

—

The cafeteria is one of those cafeterias that is also a gymnasium. Retractable bright orange basketball hoops tucked into their upright positions. Large many-paned windows far up the sides of the walls. There is no escape from a place like this.

I see many little shoes under the tables holding very still.

There is one boy lying under a chair and he is looking at me wide-eyed, as if I'd walked on stage before my cue.

That's when I see Henry.

Unlike his usual swim trunks, he is dressed in all-black. He is at the far end of the cafeteria, carrying a rifle that looks very big for him. He is aiming at something when he looks over at me.

"What are you doing here?" he hollers in a voice that is very different from the voice I remember at the pool.

"I'm here because you're here," I say.

—

No one knows what Charles Whitman's mother said to him before he stabbed her in the heart.

No one knows what the girl in the green sweater said.

Although, probably, she said nothing. I think that's the case for most people. Maybe there's only time for some facial expression or a deep breath, like you're about to dive into an alpine lake.

—

Probably, Whitman said nothing. Probably, he tried not to look at her.

—

The boy I met at a motel pool is gone, but Henry is still somehow pointing his father's rifle at me now. If he recognizes me, it doesn't register. Taco night and geometry are old news.

I am the shed marked ONLY!

I am a future data point.

Or am I Wild Bill Hickok? Wild Rog Prumont?

The sirens in the distance aren't so distant anymore.

Some of the children have scooted out from under the tables and are running behind me, leaving us.

I look out through one of the big windows near the ceiling and its unadulterated blue sky. No trees. No clouds. Zoe and I are looking up at the same sky, maybe. The same wispy white clouds. Some fathers take their daughters to Zion National Park or Saint Kitts. My daughter and I came to Little Lake, Iowa to drink Harvey Wallbangers and break into people's RVs.

What are the odds?

—

What my obituary should actually read:

```
     He was incredibly happy at the very

end.
```

Acknowledgements

I would like to thank the following people, without whom this book would not be what it is. Constance Renfrow, Samuel Douglas, and Jay Kristensen Jr., for their keen eye and encouragement along the way. Andrew Wicklund, for being a great book designer and even better friend. Everyone at Unsolicited Press, for believing in my writing, especially Summer Stewart.

I would also like to thank my wonderful family, most of all my wife, who is a better editor than I am and has been promised that my next book will not contain any marital calamities that might be construed as having anything to do with our actual lives, which are perfect in every way.

About the Author

Trevor J. Houser lives in Seattle with his family. His first novel, *Pacific*, was a finalist for the Eric Hoffer Book Award, National Indie Excellence Awards, and Next Generation Indie Book Awards.

About Unsolicited Press

Unsolicited Press is based out of Portland, Oregon and focuses on the works of the unsung and underrepresented. As a womxn-owned, all-volunteer small publisher that doesn't worry about profits as much as championing exceptional literature, we have the privilege of partnering with authors skirting the fringes of the lit world. We've worked with emerging and award-winning authors such as Shann Ray, Amy Shimshon-Santo, Brook Bhagat, Kris Amos, and John W. Bateman.

Learn more at unsolicitedpress.com. Find us on twitter and instagram.

CPSIA information can be obtained
at www.ICGtesting.com
Printed in the USA
LVHW041114190723
752815LV00006B/78